SUPER ~~~
SAVING
THE DAY!

A TOTALLY
HILARIOUS
STORY FROM
TOM MCLAUGHLIN!

CAN YOU
TRUST YOUR
**SMART
SPEAKER?**

**EEEK!!!
ROBOT
SPIDERS!!!**

TO ALEXANDER, ALL MY LOVE X

OXFORD
UNIVERSITY PRESS

Great Clarendon Street, Oxford OX2 6DP

Oxford University Press is a department of the University of Oxford.
It furthers the University's objective of excellence in research, scholarship,
and education by publishing worldwide. Oxford is a registered trade mark
of Oxford University Press in the UK and in certain other countries

British Library Cataloguing in Publication Data

Data available

ISBN: 978-0-19-276692-2

1 3 5 7 9 10 8 6 4 2

Printed in Great Britain

Paper used in the production of this book is a natural,
recyclable product made from wood grown in sustainable forests.
The manufacturing process conforms to the environmental
regulations of the country of origin.

Graph paper: Alfonso de Tomas/Shutterstock.com

Tom McLaughlin

ATTACK OF THE SMART SPEAKERS

OXFORD
UNIVERSITY PRESS

BLACK FRIDAY

'Hey you! Are you tired of
having to use your brain? Brains
aren't for thinking, brains are
to be entertained with TV, happy
music, and funny things on the
Internet! Thinking won't make
you happier, we have computers
for that! Introducing your new
virtual buddy, Nova!'

'Hey Nova, what's the best recipe for a mung bean and quinoa smoothie?'

'Hey Nova, what time does my life-coaching session start?'

'All you need to do is tell us a little bit about yourself—you know, like your shoe size, blood group, every piece of data that you've ever inputted on any computer or phone ever in your life—and you're all good to go!'

'Hey Nova, can you play my inner happiness playlist?'

'Why not have one for every room in your house, so you never have to think again!'

'Hey Nova, can you please pass the bucket, I
think I'm going to throw-up.' I add this to the
list of requests for Nova. 'We have to watch
the same advert every time. I've seen this one
probably a billion times now,' I sigh.

'Tyler, if you really had seen it a billion times,
you'd have to have been watching it since you

were approximately minus 47. Were you born minus 47 years ago?' Ashley asks.

'No, clearly it was a joke,' I reply, as we sit in front of the TV in our den waiting for our favourite programme to get going again. Dylan looks over at me and gulps nervously, waiting for Ashley's response.

'NEVER EVER JOKE ABOUT MATHS!' Ashley yells at me as if I'd somehow insulted her good family name. 'NUMBERS ARE THE ONE CONSTANT IN THIS CHAOTIC UNIVERSE. THE BEDROCK OF ALL CERTAINTY. WE ARE SCIENTISTS. WE ARE UNSHAKABLE. WE HOLD THE BUNSEN BURNER OF TRUTH. WE WEAR THE WHITE COATS OF JUSTICE. WE . . . Oh look our show has started again,' Ashley says, turning up the volume.

It's *Antiques Goldmine*. Some people have wrestling, some people have baseball, we have some mild-mannered pensioners fighting about how much their old tat may be worth on *Antiques Goldmine*. Will it be worth a few pounds, or a million? If you can find a better show that has all the drama of the World Cup Final with the reward of cold hard cash, and a bit of Greek tragedy thrown in, then I've yet to see it.

I look out from our den—a silver caravan parked in my dad's garden—and wonder how many other people in our strange town of Happyville are watching the show. I guess we're probably the only ones. Happyville's not exactly what you'd call cultured. If you're new here I should probably say a few things. Firstly, where have you been? You've missed quite a ride already. Secondly, we have had holographic-app malfunctions, people turning into werewolves—and that time arms suddenly grew 6 feet long for no apparent reason, but you can hear about that another time.

Let me introduce myself—my name is Tyler Fitz, but everyone calls me Fitz. I moved to Happyville with my dad not so long ago, after Mum . . . well, got ill and . . . you know. It's this strange town where everyone wants to be beautiful and happy. As if one makes the other possible, I mean duh! They've thought of everything here—they've found the prettiest shade of green for the lawns, worked out how many trees per person are needed to make people feel cheerful—even the flowers have been genetically modified to grow perfectly straight and neat. It's like, well, living in a Nova commercial. Fortunately, I found Ashley and Dylan. They are my saviours. While everyone else is busy whitening their teeth, or perfecting their conditioner-to-rinse ratio, we hang about and read books, talk about numbers, watch *Antiques Goldmine*—and save the world from apocalyptic near misses.

'That's got to be worth a few hundred!' Dylan says as the fusty expert runs his eye over an old oil painting.

'Nah, I'm playing my "worth half a million if it hadn't been damaged" card,' Ashley says slapping it down on the table. Yes, that's right, we've made playing cards to help make the show more interactive. The winner gets a rice cracker. It's one of the only food items that Ashley can tolerate without breaking out in hives. What topping the winner puts on the rice cracker, well that's the real prize.

'. . . and how much do you think it's worth?' the expert asks the lady whose painting it is.

'Well, I'm not really interested in selling . . .' she says, shaking her head.

'LIAR!' we all yell back.

'The mouth may say that but your eyes don't,' I shout.

The expert smiles. 'It may surprise you to know that it's—'

'**Hey you, tired of using your brain?**' The Nova ad strikes up again.

'NOO!' we all groan. 'How many more times?'

'**Get your own Nova package, with 25 per cent off this Friday!**' it continues.

'IF I BUY ONE, WILL YOU STOP?!' Dylan yells back. 'I want to see the lady be disappointed that her painting isn't worth anything! Hit the mute button Ashley . . . Ashley!' she carries on but Ashley is mesmerized by the ad.

'What?' She snaps out of it.

'Are you okay? We lost you for a second there.'

'Yes, no . . . I'm just interested in the technology. I mean it's basic, but its AI potential to learn is interesting. Mine arrived yesterday.'

'You've bought one?' I say. 'Well you kept that quiet.'

'It links to your phone via the Internet. Look!' she says, holding out the screen.

'Have you got your parents trapped in a maze?' I ask, squinting at it.

'Yes. If they get out, I give them a reward. If they make a mistake . . . well, a small electric shock gives them something to think about. I've got a couple of Novas collecting the data for me. I said it was for a science project at school. But it's not, it's all for me.'

'A "couple" of Novas?' Dylan asks. 'How many do you actually have?'

'Four . . .'

'FOUR!' we both yell.

'Oh okay, seven,' Ashley admits. 'I know, but think of the potential!'

'I am and er . . . all those things sound bad,' Dylan says.

'Yeah. No computer should know more about you than you, it's not right,' I agree.

'I'm looking at it purely from a scientific perspective. All I want is—'

'Yeah, we know. A nerd utopia with you as the emperor!' Dylan shakes her head.

'And what's wrong with that?' Ashley protests. 'Anyway, Fitz. You need to play your card, what do you think it's going to be worth?'

'Oh, right, yeah.' I look at my options. 'I'm going for, "it's a forgery and you've been had by the person who sold it to you"!' I say confidently.

'Remember, get your Nova tomorrow for Black Friday. Terms and conditions apply.'

'Welcome back viewers. We were just about to value this oil painting . . .' The *Antiques Goldmine* expert turns to the owner. 'And how does half a million sound?' he asks smugly.

'Oh, my!' The lady begins to weep.

'That's how much it *would* be worth, but I'm afraid it's been damaged. Look someone has drawn a big moustache on it.' The expert smiles, delighted with himself.

'No, no, no. That moustache is *supposed* to be there, the artist painted it on!' she says desperately.

'Madam, it's a painting of Queen Victoria. Personally, I think this is worth maybe a bag of crisps, or a used sock, at best,' he says, before punching a hole in it and kicking the thing over.

'Yes! I win!' Ashley smiles.

'Indeed you do, here's your prize.'

'Aha, the rice cracker of victory, it smells so

sweet,' Ashley says, holding it above her head like a champion.

'And what topping are you going to have on it?' I ask.

'Well, as I'm allergic to all forms of spreads, jams, and chutneys, can I have another rice cracker on top?'

'The *Ashley Special*? Yep,' I say. Just at that second, we hear a loud buzzing sound, like a giant bee has been trapped in a tiny matchbox. Except this is getting louder and louder. Suddenly the whole den goes dark, as if a giant shadow is blocking the sunshine.

'What on earth?' I say. But still the buzzing grows and grows. We look at each other, nervously. It's no good, whatever is out there, it's getting closer. We need to investigate. My tummy begins to bubble and fizz, the way it does whenever we begin an adventure. What will it be this time? I think to myself. Holographic dinosaurs, aliens from outer space, an escaped character from a virtual-reality video game? I take a deep breath and open the door of the den, it's time to see *who* or *what* is out there.

IT CAME
FROM ABOVE

'This is it. Take me to the mother ship . . . take me back to my home planet. I knew I was too smart to be a human, take me back to Planet Ashley where I belong!' Ashley says, flinging the door of the den back. 'Look, it's landing! I'M GOING HOME!' She grins as the inky shadow from above grows and swallows her. 'Ouch!'

A giant box has landed on Ashley. A split second later and a claw breaks through the box

16

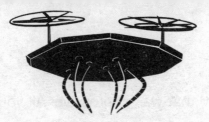

and tears a hole through it. Out falls a smiling
robot landing on top of Ashley's head.

'ARRRRRGH!' I scream. 'WE'RE UNDER
ATTACK!'

'It's just a drone delivery!' Dad calls, as he
comes round the corner.

'YOUR NOVA HAS BEEN DELIVERED!'
comes the automated voice of the drone.

'Wow, that was impressive. All you had to do was think about getting one and it arrived. I mean, it's like they can read minds,' Dylan says, picking up the box. 'Oh wait, it's not for me, it's for Tyler's dad.'

'BRIAN!' Ashley yells, plucking the Nova from the top of her hair. Ashley insists on calling Dad by his first name, which is weird and overfamiliar. A point I keep making to Ashley, which just makes her do it more.

'Oh, sorry, girls!' Dad says, coming out into the back garden. 'I had a text saying the parcel was here and I tried to land it with my smartphone, but I guess I overshot the runway and it landed in the back garden.'

'Brian, leave the flying to the professionals,'

Ashley says, rubbing her head.

'Are you in pain? Is your brain working normally? Are you making sense?' Dad asks, trying to give Ashley the once over.

'Ashley has for a long time held the belief that she is an alien species on account of her genius. She thinks it's only a matter of time until she gets plucked from Planet Earth and taken "home". Isn't that right, Ashley?' Dylan asks.

'Dylan, that was supposed to be classified information, not to be shared with any other humans,' Ashley says, through gritted teeth.

'I believe you! I went to kindergarten with a girl called Blossom. Then one day she disappeared,' Dylan explains. 'She was super smart, as well. I think she went to outer space, too.' Dylan smiles sweetly.

'If it helps, Ashley, I've always thought of you as being from another planet,' Dad tells her. 'Now, please pass the Nova to me!' He practically snatches it out of Ashley's hands, like an excited kid at Christmas. 'Isn't she beautiful?' He holds the small round speaker up to the light. 'Look, it has a little mouth so you can see it when it talks . . . Oh, and check *this* out! . . . Hey, Nova, give me five?'

A tiny little robot arm pops out and high-fives

my dad. 'It's wireless, and it'll do whatever I say: play music, put the oven on, organize my diary. It's like having a new brain. Look at my new brain!' Dad smiles.

'Er, are you sure about all this? I mean, you have to hand over a lot of personal information to get one of these. I don't think anything should have that much information, it could be . . . dangerous,' I say, looking at Dad.

'Yeah, but it's so shiny and pretty, and look at the green light. Gorgeous!' Dad beams.

'Yes, I know. But just because it looks pretty doesn't mean it's nice, I mean, look at Courtney—she's the prettiest school bully I've ever seen!'

'That's an excellent point, and well made

using the medium of humour,' Ashley says,
deadpan.

'Er, thanks,' I nod. 'But it wasn't really a
joke.'

'Look. All we do is switch it on. Nothing
bad comes from hitting this trigger button.
Triggers aren't bad,' Dad says, enthusiastically.

'Everything bad comes from triggers!' I yell.

'Hello, I am Nova, your
virtual guardian. Would you like
me to connect to your Wi-Fi?'

'YES!' Dad claps giddily.

'Would you please grant me
access to your and everyone in
your household's life?'

'YEEES!' He giggles.

'You are agreeing to terms
and conditions?'

'Oh, yes.'

'Would you like me to read
you the terms and conditions?'

'NAH!' Dad grins.

'Shoe size?'

'Eleven!'

'Come on, Brian,' Ashley says looking
down at my dad's feet.

'Okay. Nine-and-a-half.'

'Blood type?'

'Red!'

'I now have complete access
to your entire life. I have

turned the house lights down and ordered your favourite pizza. There was a discount voucher that needed using up—I hope that's okay, Brian? Tyler, your homework is due in tomorrow, I just thought you should know. Ashley, your dinner will be ready in twenty minutes, so you'd better leave now.'

'My dinner? How do you know that?' Ashley frowns.

'I am connected to all other Novas in Happyville in order to bring you the ultimate in guardian protection. And Dylan . . .?'

'Yes?' Dylan replies eagerly.

`I really like ribbons and unicorns too,'` Nova says.

'Oh, gee Nova . . .' Dylan gushes.

'Wow. I have to admit that's impressive,' I say.

'It's pretty good, right?' Dad grins. 'Although, Nova, if you keep getting me pizza, I will start to get a bit—'

`'Nonsense. You're in great shape Brian. Your body mass index is below 20 per cent, which is great for a man of your age. That aside, I have the perfect spin class routine for you to begin in the morning—it's`

a great way to begin the day and
get you in the mood to start
that book you've been trying to
write. I hope you don't mind,
but I have made you a schedule
to help you structure your day
so you can get the most out of
it,' Nova says, in her sickly-sweet robot
voice.

Getting Dad writing and keeping fit?
Maybe I was wrong? Maybe this isn't such a
bad idea?

'Good morning, Tyler, how are
you today?'

'Wow, that pizza was delicious last night . . . '
I mutter, beginning to wake up. The gentle
sound of ocean waves crashing fills the air.
I open my eyes.

'ARRRRGH!!!' I yell, looking at the Nova
grinning away at me, not 2 inches from my nose
on the bedside table. 'WHO LET YOU IN?!'

'Ah, there you are!' Dad appears, scooping
up the Nova. 'I knew I'd put this down
somewhere. Must've been when I came in to
kiss you goodnight last night.'

'Oh, I see. Dad, what are you wearing?' I
ask, trying not to be creeped out by the fact
a robot's been watching me sleep all night
and that my dad seems to be dressed in shiny
sportswear.

'Are you not going to say good morning to Nova?' he asks.

'Er, okay . . . Good morning, Nova. Are you . . . well?' I ask. Maybe a silly question, as it's a computer and has no idea what being 'well' feels like, but it just feels rude not to ask.

'I am a computer, Tyler, I have no idea what being well feels like. The question is silly,' Nova replies. 'But everything within my operating system is functioning perfectly, thank you for asking. There's an antiques show on later that I've added to your wish list'

'That's lovely, thank you. But seriously, Dad,

what are you wearing?' I ask as he potters around my room, tidying up. Why do parents love to potter?

I reach over to the bedside table for my glasses. As the blurry world comes into focus, I have a clearer view of Dad in a full Lycra bodysuit, complete with sweatband and leggings. It is, unsurprisingly, one of the worst sights there is to see. 'What's going on, Dad, why are you so . . . sh*iny*?'

'I've been doing exercise!' he puffs. 'I'm part of a community spin class now.

I didn't have an exercise bike so I took the wheels off yours, I hope that's okay. We are all trying do our bit in the neighbourhood, all of us in Happyville. Through a Nova-connect each morning, we do a work out together. That way we're all supporting each other. I've just beaten Mrs Dobson from down the road in the four kilometre sprint!'

'Congrats, Dad. You beat an eighty-seven-year-old in a race,' I say.

'Thanks, Tyler!' He beams. 'Come and get breakfast when you're ready,' he adds, practically skipping out of my room, carrying his Nova like it's a pedigree cat.

I throw on some clothes and head to the kitchen where I'm greeted by the low sound of tinny dance music, and enough chopped fruit and vegetables to feed an army. 'What are you listening to and what are you cooking?'

'It's a new playlist. Nova thought it would suit my inner biometric rhythms. This is a full tasting low-fat breakfast smoothie,' he says, handing me a glass of green liquid sludge. 'I didn't want to undo all that spinning! It's a new recipe from . . . '

'Nova?' I suggest, deadpan. 'Dad, I have a question. Do you think maybe Nova—'

'Yes?' Nova replies.

'I wasn't talking to you.'

'Oh, sorry, I thought I heard my name. I'm always ready to listen.'

'Well, yes I did say Nova but . . . Oh, never mind. Dad, can I have a word in private?' Grabbing my smoothie I march towards the front door.

I realize that I'm dragging Dad outside onto the street, where people might see him dressed like Lady Gaga, but this is serious. 'Do you think that Happyville is relying on Novas too much?' I look around at all the other houses in the street. I can see through their windows people dressed similarly to Dad, all preparing breakfast, or dancing around.

I take a nervous sip of my smoothie. 'My WORD this is surprisingly delicious!' I say, taking another slurp. 'But that's beside the point. Don't you think that this many Novas all in one town, is a bit . . . odd?' I lift my eyes to the sky, which is littered with tiny, black drones. More Novas preparing to drop into people's homes.

'I think Happyville is just a bit of an early adopter of this sort of thing. We're like the old pioneers!'

'But—'

'Look, does your smoothie not taste delicious?' he asks.

'Yes, it's just—'

'Has Nova not made a big difference to our lives since she arrived?'

'Well, it's only been nine hours, but maybe . . . a little *too much* difference,' I say, staring at his Lycra ensemble.

'Listen. It's not easy just the two of us. You know, not since Mum . . . Well, I try my best but sometimes I need help. It's just a computer. If you give her a chance, you'll get to like her too, I'm sure.' Dad smiles.

Now I feel bad.

'Okay, maybe you're right.' I smile. 'But I have to go and get—'

`'Tyler's school bus will be here in 30 seconds.'` Dad's watch jumps in.

'I synced it up.' Dad beams. 'Now Nova is everywhere!'

I give him a hug and grab my school bag.
Maybe I'm worrying about nothing.

'Don't forget your antiques
show later, Tyler,' Nova says.

'Okay, thanks,' I say reluctantly.

'I know it's your favourite,'
she adds.

'Bye Dad!' I say, waving him off. Maybe
I'm being silly, I mean it's nice that she knows
what my favourite show is . . . Wait, how does
she know? She arrived after it had finished.
And she knew about Dylan liking ribbons and
unicorns. Always ready to listen, or *always
listening*? I say to myself, very quietly in my
head.

GLITCH IN THE MATRIX

I climb aboard the school bus and spot Ashley
and Dylan in our usual seats. There is a clear
and precise order to sitting on a bus. The cool
kids are right at the back. Probably because
it's the place furthest away from the driver,
or any teacher who may be along for the
ride. The cool kids, or 'Alphas', are the most
important and influential of any school group.
They decide who's cool, who's acceptable,

and who's a nerd. They are like an eighteenth-century royal family, making the rules and decreeing to their subjects. They get the best of everything. They rule the school. The 'Wannabes' (also known as the 'Suck-ups') are the next group down. They sit *near* the back, hoping to get invited in to join the Alphas. They try and join in when they can, helping the Alphas carry out their evil work. Occasionally one of the Wannabes joins the Alphas, if they are considered worthy. The next level down are the 'Perfectos'—they are close to Wannabe status, but too kind-hearted to be mean, the sort who don't realize that in order to climb the greasy ranks of popularity at school, you need to tread on others to get there. All in all, there's probably about five or six more sub-sections. They sit in ascending order: most popular at the back, gradually getting more and more unpopular the nearer you get to the front seats. These seats are reserved for the nerds and the teachers. That's where I find Ashley and Dylan. I sit down quickly behind them.

'I think we have a situation,' I say quietly. Ashley and Dylan turn round and look at me.

'You mean another mystery to solve?' Ashley asks.

'Oh goody! I love it when we do this. You need to do the secret signal!' Dylan grins.

'What? No I don't, I've just told you that we have a situation. That should be all the signal you need,' I whisper.

'Come on. Batman has the bat signal, we need one too,' Dylan says.

I sigh. We tried the bat thing once and it didn't work out. It turns out that waiting till nightfall to turn on a huge searchlight wasn't that convenient. So that's why we invented our new 'secret' signal.

'But that's for when we're sneaking around trying to stay hidden,' I mutter. 'I'm not sure the secret signal works in this context.'

'It's in the rules,' Dylan insists.

'It is, actually,' Ashley says, pulling them out of her bag.

'I'm not sure having our gang rules typed up and laminated is very, well, gang-like,' I say, with an eye roll.

'Yeah, but laminating is so much fun. Look, I laminated my lunch,' Ashley says, now pulling out her gluten-and-dairy-and-filling-free plastic-covered sandwich. 'Oops, I shouldn't have turned around. Motion sickness. I NEED A BAG!' She gulps.

'Here,' I say, passing her one. You soon realize that you don't go anywhere with Ashley and Dylan without carrying a supply of small sick bags. A lesson I learned the hard way on the field trip to the cheese factory last spring. 'As I was saying . . .'

'A-HEM!' Dylan is staring at me.

'Fine!' I snap. I put my hand to my mouth and hoot like an owl: our secret signal, which sounds perfect if you're creeping round the forest at night, but when you're on a crowded school bus, it sounds ridiculous, not to mention that it's no longer a secret. The entire bus stops what they're doing and stares at me. Then there is a very short silence before the hurling starts—and I don't mean from Ashley's face, I mean apples, paper aeroplanes, anything to hand that can be chucked at my head, along with, 'NERD, GEEK, OWL FACE, DORK, OWLY DORK, BIRD NERD, GEEKY CHOPS'.

You get the idea.

'Well that went well,' I whisper, when the yelling dies down. 'I think we may need to rethink the secret mystery-solving signal. Perhaps we should just start a WhatsApp group or something instead?'

'Good idea,' says Ashley.

'Yep,' Dylan agrees.

They start picking popcorn and apple debris out of their hair.

'So. What did you want to talk about?' Dylan asks.

'All these Novas . . .' I begin. 'Listen, something weird happened, it knows stuff about me.'

'Duh, that's the point,' Ashley sighs. 'You give it all your info and it helps run your life. All you have to do is grant it access to everything there is to know about you. I bought a couple more yesterday. I now have one for each room of my house, just like the advert advised.'

'So, basically, we will become a planet of

humans controlled by robots,' I put in, but no one is listening.

'My family got their Nova yesterday,' Dylan is saying. 'It made me eat fruit for breakfast. I mean, fruit? No one eats fruit deliberately. Fruit is the thing that you eat to get to the good part— sweets and chocolate. But Nova won't let me eat any chocolate. I like chocolate. Do you have any chocolate? I *really* want some chocolate . . . what were we talking about again?'

'Nova is taking the human out of the human race and personally I think it's great. Look, Nova is controlling my parents as we speak.' Ashley pulls out her phone and shows the view from the Nova webcams that she has scattered around her house.

'It's good to see you've let them out of the maze. Do your parents know you keep an eye on them while you're out?' I ask, peering at the sight of Ashley's mum and dad vacuuming, whilst simultaneously doing an aerobics routine *and* cooking breakfast.

'Where's the fun in that? As a scientist you need to stand back and observe. You don't tell a lab rat what you want it to do, do you?'

'To be fair, they're not rats, they're your parents,' Dylan says taking a look.

'Until I'm old enough to be able to get a DNA test to prove that theory one way or the other, I'm going to carry on with the experiment,' Ashley tells her.

'The experiment being?' I ask.

'The experiment *being* to control the human guardians who claim to be related to me. I intend to bring the system down from within. Just because society has decided that I as a child need to be controlled by adults doesn't mean it's right. It's about flipping the paradigm.'

'Why did you have to get her going on this again?' Dylan whispers to me.

'I'm so sorry . . . ' I smile weakly.

'And the sooner the robots are in control the better!' Ashley smiles.

'Great. Anyway, my point is that I think we need to work out what's going on with these machines. I have a feeling that they're listening to us all the time, even when they're dormant. I mean has anyone actually read the terms and conditions?' I say quietly. 'I just think we need to be careful and make sure that we don't surround ourselves with too many of them.'

At this point, the bus pulls to a juddering halt and the doors open.

'STOPPING AT MAIN STREET. THE NEXT STOP, HAPPYVILLE HIGH SCHOOL. THE WORLD'S FIRST NOVA-RUN SCHOOL!' The now familiar sound of Nova's voice comes over the speaker.

'Agh!' I yelp. 'A Nova school and by the looks of it a Nova bus! What is wrong with this town? This is—'

'Awful. I can't stand Nova, I mean who does she think she is?' comes another familiar voice, only this time a human one. 'Hello nerdlings,' says Courtney, the prettiest school bully, climbing aboard.

Yep. The worst part about sitting near the front is people getting on and walking straight past you, normally accompanied by some sort of sarcastic comment.

But Courtney stops, hovering in front of me. 'Wait, what were you going to say?' she says looking at me.

'I was going to say, it's awful, too . . .' I mumble.

'Well you would say that, wouldn't . . . Wait, are we agreeing on something?' Courtney gives me a look of confusion.

'Yes, I believe we are.'

We stare at each other for a second. This

has never happened before. Normally, Courtney says the opposite of everything I say. She is my exact mirror image in every way. We never agree on anything. I don't know what to do. This is the unstoppable object meeting the unmovable force, as Isaac Newton predicted.

'I don't understand,' we both say at the same time.

'Whoa!' Dylan and Ashley gasp. 'I think there's a glitch in the matrix.' The bus goes quiet as everyone takes in what's happening.

'Courtney, what's going on? Why are you talking like the nerds?' Tiffany yells. Tiffany is Courtney's second-in-command. As in, she's her deputy. If Courtney's a can of Bully, Tiffany is a can of Bully-Lite.

'I'm not talking like the nerds. I just don't like the Nova, that's all, Tiffany.' Courtney sighs.

'What? Everyone likes the Nova, except the nerds. If you don't like it, I guess that makes you a nerd!' Tiffany gasps.

'Classic,' Ashley mutters, shaking her head. 'Confusing cause with correlation.'

'I am not a nerd, you doofus. Look at me. Would a nerd team cashmere with satin? Honestly, Tiffany. We'll talk about this at your appraisal next week. I had a lot of people apply to be my deputy you know?'

'Sorry. You and Tyler just sounded like friends, that's all.' Tiffany shakes her head from the back of the bus.

'We're *not* friends,' Courtney and I say at the

same time.

'Wow. It's like you're twins!' Dylan smiles.

'Shut up. Clearly, there is a mistake. I don't like the Nova, so clearly you must like it, because it's a computer and your people like computers.' She wafts her arm at us.

'*Your people?*' Dylan asks.

'Geeks, she means geeks,' I reassure her. 'I do like computers, but—'

'But you don't like Nova?' Courtney asks.

`'Hello, I'm here to help!'` Nova butts in.

'Hush!' Courtney and I say.

'Why don't you like Nova?' I ask. 'Nova will organize your diary, feed you smoothies full of pointless ingredients that they pretend detox you.

They encourage the wearing of ridiculous Lycra outfits . . .'

'I know, I like those smoothies, it's just—' Courtney wrinkles her nose.

'Just what?' Ashley asks.

'No computer should know too much about anyone,' Courtney and I say at exactly the same time. AGAIN.

'Okay, this is getting spooky,' Dylan chuckles.

'I'm sorry, I can't do this,' Courtney says. 'Open the bus doors, I'm getting off.'

'Er, you can't get off the bus just because you and Fitz are sisterz from other misterz,' Dylan chuckles. 'No seriously, maybe you're related? You know, for realsies.'

'Let me off this bus!' Courtney cries. The

bus door finally opens and she gives me a very confused look before getting off.

'Well, that was strange. You two saying the same thing and agreeing. Maybe she's a genius now, or perhaps you're an empty-hearted, selfish prom queen, Fitz?' Ashley shrugs at me.

The rest of the journey is spent in silence and then we're at school.

'Meet me at breaktime, in the library,' I whisper to them as we disembark. 'We need to work out what's going on. Nothing about this day is making sense.'

'Goodbye,' the Nova says cheerily, as each child gets off. 'Goodbye, have a good day. Goodbye, work hard. Stay amazing. Goodbye Tyler, have a good day.'

'Wait, what, did you say my name?' I ask. 'Did you hear her say my name?' I ask the other two.

'Goodbye. Goodbye, have a good day. You're amazing.' The voice carries on.

'It must have been your imagination,' Ashley says. 'The Nova on the bus can't know our names.'

'Did you hear it, Dylan?' I ask. 'Dylan?'

'Chocolate!' Dylan says pulling her head out of her bag. 'I knew there was some in here. Did you say something, Fitz?'

'Er . . . no, it's fine. It must just be my imagination,' I mutter. 'It must be all in my head.'

TERMS AND
CONDITIONS APPLY

'Hello, kids. Welcome to the world's first official Nova School.'

There, stood by the gates in his denim suit, is Mr Jones the headmaster. We all stop to listen.

'Yes, that's right, kids. Welcome to what I can officially say is the world's first and only computerized school. All thanks to our new sponsorship deal with Nova!' He beams at us.

'I know, it's officially hashtag amazeballs, right?
I've basically been replaced by a computer.
Isn't that exciting, kids?'

I don't think he knows that being replaced
by a computer is a bad thing.

'It'll mean I have more time to
spend working on my other
career as an actor-stroke-
model.' Mr Jones
smiles, running his
fingers through his
suspiciously thick
hair. 'Now, I don't want
you to worry. It's not like a
computer will be doing any
of the *important* stuff, like

photography or fashion or yoga or anything like that. Just the other things, like maths, and science, and . . . well, you know, the *boring* things, the stuff that the nerds like—no offence to you Tyler, and Ashley, and Dylan . . . and all the other nerdlings.' Mr Jones chuckles.

'Boring?' Dylan says, hurt. 'Are we boring?'

'No, we're just right the way we are,' I say. 'And there's no way we should be taught by robots. That's not how school works.'

'Look, I think you two are being babies about this. A school run by algorithmic Artificial Intelligence! This is the dream!' Ashley smiles, but there's a strange vacant look in her eye.

'Look, just meet me later in the library to talk things through. I think we need to be careful here, something just doesn't feel right about all this,' I whisper to my friends.

'So enjoy your new future, kids!' booms Mr Jones. 'If you have any questions, your new virtual teacher Nova will be able to help! Now, it's time to go get a spray tan!' This is met by loud cheers from many of the assembled pupils. 'No, no!' Mr Jones frowns. '*I'm* the one getting the spray tan, *you're* all going to class.' This is obviously met by rumbles of discontent.

I look at Ashley and Dylan. Ashley looks all wide-eyed, like someone who just found her spirit animal, except that her spirit animal is a small round computer called Nova. Dylan and I look at each other and gulp, then head into school. For every other kid in the place, having a robot take care of everything for you is the dream. It means you can disengage your brain and let someone else or something else take over. It means that you can think about more important things, such as the latest music release, or how to wear your trousers, and is purple the new green or is it the new black?

I skulk into school, and everything seems shinier and more sterile than normal. I poke my head through a classroom door. A Nova proudly sits on the desk, taking the register, while a teacher sits at the back of the class, painting her nails.

'I'll see you both later,' I say to Ashley and Dylan. 'And remember, the library at lunchtime. Ter-wit ter-woo!' I hoot like an owl for good measure.

'I agree with the terms and conditions!' a voice booms. I turn round to see the school caretaker, just one in a long line of school staff who are buying into this nonsense.

'That is not how an owl hoots,' I hear a female voice say, seemingly from nowhere. 'It's a common misconception that owls go ter-wit ter-woo. Actually, one owl goes ter-wit while the other owl in the pair goes woo. Now hurry along to class.'

'WHERE IS THAT COMING FROM?!' I say, looking around, wildly. 'It's like she's in my head!'

'I think . . .' Dylan says, looking at Ashley's bag. 'I think it's coming from in there?'

'Ashley?' I say, annoyed.

'I don't have one in my bag.' Ashley shrugs. 'Oh really. Well I hope you're telling the truth, because we know what happens when you lie. It's all aboard the puke train, last stop Toiletsville,' I say, pulling out another sick bag.

'I don't need that!' Ashley laughs. 'I feel absolutely fi—eughhh. Okay, I admit it. I brought one of mine in today. Hey Nova. What's the 479th digit in the maths equation of pi?' she asks.

`'Eight,'` comes the smug reply.

'Ha, correct!'

'Hey Nova. Can we carry on our game of twelve-dimensional chess?' she asks.

`'Sure Ashley,'` says Nova. `'But first I want you to get me something . . .'`

I stare as Dylan and Ashley start wandering off together with Nova still talking.

'Don't forget we're meeting in the library

later,' I yell after them.

'You have a fitness class later, Tyler,' another Nova voice calmly calls out.

'Argh!' I look up at the ceiling. They're everywhere, all around me! 'How do you know my name?'

'We all know your name, Tyler,' several Novas reply at the same time. Their echo bounces off the walls, round the corridor, and back to me. 'Don't fight us,' they add.

'WHAAA!' I cry in fright. 'I need to get out of here!' I run towards the cafeteria, but the door closes in front of me.

'No, Tyler,' a voice says, it's from

a small Nova attached to the door. I turn and
run back the other way, bumping into everyone
as I go, through a maze of corridors, and then
I'm lost, disorientated. I don't know where I am.
People and Novas are all talking at me. I can't
breathe. It's like Nova is controlling everyone and
everything. Desperately, I grab at another door.

'Let me out. LET ME OUT!' I yell.

'No Tyler!' The door yells back at me.

'YOU'RE NOT IN CHARGE, NOVA. YOU CAN'T TELL ME WHAT TO DO!'

'YOU MUST OBEY ME, TYLER! I AM IN CHARGE OF YOU!' The door barks back at me. Nova's gentle tones are gone. It's now a battle between girl and machine.

'Open the door, Nova. I am a human, I am in charge. You work for me.'

'NO!'

'YES!'

'NO!'

'What's going on here?' Mr Jones appears beside me.

'I just need some air. I think I'm going to puke,' I say, trying to think of something convincing to say.

'Open the door, Nova. We certainly don't want any puking,' Jones says.

'Of course, sir,' Nova replies, sweetly.

'You see, all you need to do is ask nicely and Nova will obey.' He smiles at me like I'm an idiot.

'She wouldn't listen,' I try to explain.

'She? It has no gender, Tyler. It's just Nova.' He smiles.

'I know, but . . .'

'Well, it seems to be working now, anyway'
he says, opening the door and letting in the
warm air. Finally, I can breathe again.

'Oh, Mr Jones,' Nova says,'can
we have more data on the
children? The more we know
the better we become. I just
need you to grant me access to
their lives.'

'*More* data?' I say, breathing in the air.
'How much do you need? You already know all
our names.'

'Oh come on now, Tyler, the more data you
give Nova, the more it can do,' says Mr Jones.
'It's like painting with all the colours. Think of

data like a big pallet. The more colours the better.' For a second I think about reminding him of Picasso's blue period, but it doesn't feel like the right time.

'That's very true, it's all in my terms and conditions, which you've already agreed to,' Nova says. 'The more colour the better, the more data the better. Talking of which, that's a lovely shade of mahogany, Mr Jones.'

'Thanks. It's my new spray tan.' He smiles.

'But how did you find the time to get a spray tan?' I ask. 'You were here literally ten minutes ago.'

'I've got one in my office,' Mr Jones smiles. 'All controlled by—'

'Let me guess. Nova,' I say, rolling my eyes. Then an idea pops into my head, 'Nova?' I ask, politely. 'Did you say something about terms and conditions? What exactly are they?' I put my hand in my pocket and grab my phone.

'Well, seeing as you asked, Tyler . . .' Nova begins to spout out a long list of terms and conditions at what feels like a thousand words a minute. Too fast for me to decipher in the moment. But maybe when I slow down the recording on my phone later . . .? I smile to myself. Now, that's a whole different story.

PERMS AND CONDITIONERS APPLY

'Listen to this!' I pull out my phone and hit play.

'Is that a whale singing perms and conditioners apply?' Dylan asks.

'Nope, it's the Nova's terms and conditions . . .' I whisper.

'You don't need to whisper, Tyler. There are no Novas in here, I checked. No one ever uses the library.'

'Okay. Well, I recorded Nova reciting the

terms and conditions on my phone earlier. But she speaks so quickly that I couldn't make head nor tail of it, so I slowed the playback down. Listen.'

'Nice work!' Dylan smiles.

'Listen to this bit.' I say, fast forwarding.

'Once you've agreed to the terms and conditions, I will have access to all your data, and that of every single person you know. I have permission to use and share your personal data from your past digital footprint with anyone. I now own everything about you. I have permission to listen to you even when switched off. I have permission to rule over you how I see fit. By agreeing to these terms and conditions you are handing me everything . . .' the Nova recording chants.

'No wonder the Nova knows everything about me,' I tell Dylan. 'Dad agreed to the terms and conditions without even knowing what they were, and now Nova knows everything about me. It's like a ripple, always growing, taking everyone's personal information!'

'Whoa. That doesn't sound good. How come nobody knows about this?'

'Because people don't ever read the terms

and conditions. My dad granted his Nova access. I bet yours did, too,' I say, then look at my watch. 'By the way, where's Ashley? She should be here.'

'She's getting changed. You know how she feels about communal changing rooms so she's gone to hide in a cupboard to get her gym kit on.'

'Why?' I say. 'Gym class isn't until Wednesday. You know, the day when we all come down with that mysterious illness that means we had to stay home and pretend to be ill while actually doing extra maths!' I say.

'Oh, haven't you heard?' Dylan sighs

'Heard what?'

'Communal dance?' I say to Dylan and Ashley, as we head out to the sports field ten minutes later.

'*Communal* and *dance* are two words that should never be put together, like *karaoke* and *competition*, or *organized* and *fun*. It's just wrong.'

'Did you not get the updated timetable? Nova sent them all round this morning,' Ashley says, pointing at her watch.

'No I did not,' I sigh.

'Where did you go? The last time I saw you, you were running down the corridor,' Ashley asks.

'I just had to get out of there, you know. I needed some air. Having the entire computer

74

network in the school shout my name in a creepy way was somewhat overwhelming. You know what I mean?' I tell them.

'Well, there's plenty of air outside.' Ashley beams at me.

'Yes, thank you, Ashley.'

'A quadrillion square tons in this part of the world alone,' she continues. 'So, you know, you should be safe.'

We head out joined by the rest of the school, who all clearly got the memo too, unlike me. The Lycra dazzles my eyes in the sun. Teachers and pupils alike, all stretching and limbering up for what I can only assume will involve things like coordination, pop music, and keeping in time—all of which I'm bad at.

'Why do we never come out and do communal maths, or chant about the joys of the periodic table?' I ask.

There, at the top of the sports field, on the podium normally reserved for champions, sits a Nova in front of a microphone, which is connected to the speakers around the sports field.

'Fitz, I'm scared, Fitz.' Dylan clutches my arm.

'We all are,' I say.

'You know how I feel about sport. It's not good, it makes me blotchy. I go blotchy under stress,' Dylan says, checking her face for hives.

'It's going to be fine, we all know the drill,' I reassure her.

'Stand in the corner and hope that no one spots us when we sneak off?' Ashley recites our standard plan for anything sport or activity related at school.

'Yep,' I smile, then lean into Ashley. 'Listen, I need to talk to you. It's about—'

'**HELLO!**' yells the Nova.

'NOVA!' The entire school yells back,

including Ashley.

'What do you want to talk to me about?'
Ashley whispers, then.

'Never mind,' I say. 'It can wait.'

**'Everyone form a giant
circle,'** Nova yells out.

'A circle. Fitz, circles don't have corners!'
Dylan begins to panic at the obstacle to our
plan. 'That's what makes them not squares!' She
backs away from the crowd.

'Don't go, Dylan. The Nova's so beautiful.'
Ashley smiles goofily.

'Ash?!' I say, looking at her, but it's like
she's in a trance. Her eyes are spinning like a
couple of saucers on a roundabout. I look over
at Dylan, and she looks back at me, equally

puzzled by Ashley's weird behaviour. 'Ashley!'
I yell again.

'Come, join in, Fitz and Dylan. Be part of the future!' she grins.

'Since there's no hiding in the corner, we need a plan B. We are three, well, two geniuses,' I say, looking over at Ash who's staring giddy-eyed at the machine. 'We can find a way to get through this.'

'I mean, sure. I could build a small but viable nuclear reactor out of the contents of Ashley's bag.' Dylan gulps. 'But when it comes to dancing, I'm stuck.'

'Yeah, but to be fair, Ashley probably has a small nuclear reactor in her bag anyway.'

'How else do you think I get through the

day without having to charge my smartwatch? The battery's a killer.' Ashley shrugs.

'Are you ready, Happyville High?!' Nova starts.

Too late. 'Drat,' I say. 'We're trapped.'

'Thank you for coming to the first session of what will become part of our new daily routine. Now, before we begin, who here had one of our super-duper healthy smoothies for breakfast?' There's a loud cheer from the kids and teachers. Including Ashley too. I shoot her a look and she looks back as if to say, 'so what?'.

'Are we all ready for today's keep fit dance class? I can see you're in your sportswear . . . '

'Stop spying on me!' I cry.

'I wish I couldn't see,' Dylan says, her
eyes filled with horror at the sight of Mr Jones
galloping his way on to the field.

'So *that's* why he went to get a spray tan,'
Ashley says blinking. 'I didn't know you could
get speedos made of denim?'

'They're pretty tough to get hold of,'
Mr Jones says, overhearing Ashley as he jogs
past. 'These shorts are so special that they're
illegal in 48 countries.' He grins and waves
as he makes his way to the centre of the
communal circle.

'After THREE,' Nova starts.

I look around, there is no escape, there's

no way I can get out of it. There's going to
be dancing, in broad daylight—and I am
surrounded by people who can actually dance.

'TWO!' Some music starts and everyone
cheers.

I knew it. I knew they'd all know what
the song was. I haven't got a clue. It's one
of those songs that comes with a dance. It
sounds vaguely familiar, like it's on an advert
for a phone, or a fizzy drink or something. It's
like turning up to an exam and realizing that
everyone else has been revising and you've read
the wrong book. They seem to already know the
rhythms and beats, even the teachers. I haven't
felt more out of my depth since the time I took
a wrong turn in a department store and found

myself amongst the make-up and frilly dresses.

'**ONE!**' Nova shouts. The crowd begin to sway and bounce to the music. I look over at Dylan, I can see her face begin to swell as the full horror of what is happening dawns on her. Ashley is doing the moves, but she looks like a foal trying to stamp out a small fire. I try to join in by following Ashley's lead, but I soon realize following someone who doesn't know what they're doing isn't the best idea.

'`To the left, now to the right, and CLAP,`' says Nova. We all do it, even me, or at least I try.

'Do what to the left?' I yell. 'My left or your left? We're in a circle; what's the constant that we need to use as reference. I look up to the sky hoping to see the North Star. Maybe I can use the stars to direct my aerobics?

'**Just lose yourself to the music,**' Nova booms.

'Oh I'm lost all right. Argh!' I shout, but it's no good, the thumping music is so loud that it's useless—on the sports field no one can hear you scream. Am I going to the left or right, or just losing myself in the music? I need instructions. 'Ashley, Ashley, what are you doing?' I say, pulling her towards me.

'What?' she yells back.

'You're . . . you're joining in!' I cry out in disbelief. 'Why aren't you throwing up? Throwing up is normally what happens when you see jiggling in sportswear.

84

'I don't know, I just don't feel anything right now apart from a desire to dance.' Ashley shrugs.

'But what about your allergies?'

'Maybe Nova was right, maybe they're all in my head,' Ashley says.

`'And everyone, close your eyes and bop! Feel alive!'` Nova commands.

Now's our chance. I grab Dylan by the shoulder, she opens her eyes.

'Let's run!' I yell. 'Ashley, come on. Now's our chance!'

'No!' she yells back. 'I'm having fun. I like it!'

If this was an old-fashioned film I would have smacked her round the chops or wafted some smelling salts under her nose. But this is real life and I don't have any smelling salts. I make do by yelling 'WHAA!' at her face. It doesn't work. 'It's like I don't even know you anymore!' I cry. 'Ashley, we're a gang, we need you, you need to snap out of this!' I look helplessly over at Dylan.

'We can't just leave,' Dylan gulps.

'We don't have any choice. Ashley!' I yell trying to wake her again. 'Ashley, are you coming with us?' But she just keeps dancing. 'Now's our only chance, Dylan. It's got to be now. Let's go!'

We look around one more time to check the coast is clear and run, I look over my shoulder as we sprint towards the woods at the side of the sports field. Well, I say sprint, but it's more of a quick walk. As I turn round I see the sight, the strange and upsetting sight of Nova commanding the entire school. She has them in the palm of her circuit board. She can make them do anything she wants. Move a certain way, eat a certain thing. It's as awesome as it is terrifying.

'I have a question,' Dylan puffs out, as we run to the trees.

'What?' I ask.

'Where on earth are we going?'

IF YOU GO DOWN TO
THE WOODS TODAY . . .

'Fitz. FITZ!' Dylan yells out.

'What?' I snap.

'Where are we?'

'The woods,' I say.

'Yes, I can see that. The trees are a bit of a clue.'

'Well then, you know as much as me.' After running away from the sports field we find ourselves trudging through the forest at the edge of the school.

'What's the plan? Surely we didn't just run away from school—which is probably a felony, by the way—in order to end up out here with no plan of action.'

'Don't worry about school, Dylan. So we miss a day? We're still smarter than everyone else at school put together,' I tell her.

'I don't like it in here. They say that things happen in these here woods,' Dylan mumbles.

I stop dead in my tracks and turn round slowly. 'What things?' I ask.

'Well, remember Blossom, that girl I went to school with? We used to play in these woods, and one day there were bright lights in the sky and a noise overhead. I ran away, but

Blossom, well, she never made it out. I don't know what happened to her. I think that she . . . you know . . . went *home*,' Dylan says looking up.

'So this is what you meant by saying you'd "seen things"? As a scientist, I'm very disappointed in you. You're saying that your best friend was an alien. I'm going to stick my neck out here and say that she probably wasn't.'

'But what about the lights, the noise? Where did she go?' Dylan asks.

'I don't know. But probably not to Mars or Venus.' I let out a big sigh, stop, and sit on the nearest tree trunk. 'We need to wake up the population of Happyville. It's sleepwalking into disaster. We can't have the entire town under the control of robots. If they know everything about us, how long before they're totally controlling us?' I sigh, taking a breath.

'Okay, but where are we going? And what about Ashley? We shouldn't have left her behind.'

'I know, but, well, I think you have to accept something. Ashley is gone, Ashley is—'

'What?' Dylan asks, looking nervous.

'Ashley is one of *them* now.'

'No!' Dylan cries out. 'How can you say that?'

'You saw the way she was acting. You saw her dancing. I tell you, she's not herself.'

Dylan nods. 'The dancing. I forgot about the dancing.'

'Exactly. Ashley doesn't dance—it's completely out of character. It's like she was just doing it to fit in, and Ashley never fits in. Ashley is DEAD!'

'WHAT?!' Dylan howls.

'Metaphorically,' I clarify. 'If Nova can do that to Ashley, what's next? Making us play sport, or enjoy shopping? Forcing us to wear pretty dresses!'

'Ugh!' Dylan gasps. 'Well what are we going to do? We'll never save the world if we don't work as a team. I mean, this is Happyville, weird stuff happens all the time, and a town being enslaved by robots definitely counts as one of those times,' she says. 'How are we going to save the world when we are

33.333333333 per cent recurring down from the full team?!' Dylan is now starting to panic.

'Hmm. You're right. Those Novas seem to have a hold over people. They're craving more and more data, it's like a virus. They won't be happy until they've gobbled up everyone and everything. Once this town is under their control, they'll move to the next town and the next, until—'

'THEY TAKE OVER THE WORLD!' Dylan shouts. 'HUMANITY IS DOOMED. WE'LL BE SLAVES TO THESE THINGS. THEY'LL MAKE US DO SPIN CLASSES, AND TO DO THAT WE'LL HAVE TO HAVE THE RIGHT SPORTSWEAR. BUT IT WON'T STOP THERE— WE'LL NEED THE RIGHT PLAYLIST, SO WE'LL

HAVE TO SUBSCRIBE TO THE ONE THAT'S
COMPATIBLE WITH THE NOVA—AND THE
NOVA WATCH, WHEN THAT COMES OUT!
BUY THIS, BUY THAT. LOOK LIKE THIS, WEAR
THAT. LIKE AN EVIL PERSONAL SHOPPER
TELLING US ALL WHAT TO LIKE SO WE CAN
SPEND MORE ON THINGS WE'LL NEVER
NEED! THAT'S WHY WE NEED THE THREE
OF US BACK TOGETHER. WE ARE A TRICYCLE
MISSING A WHEEL. WE ARE A LETTUCE LEAF
SHORT OF A BLT—THREE, AS THEY SAY, IS
THE MAGIC NUMBER!'

Dylan is now so wound up, she's practically
hyperventilating.

'I get it! I get it!' I yell. 'We need Ashley
back.'

'How? What's the playbook here? How are we going to sort this? We are going to sort this aren't we? Fitz, tell me it's going to be okay? FITZ!'

'Dylan!' I snap. 'You're doing an awful lot of talking and you need to calm down.'

'I talk when I'm panicking. I also eat. Do you have food?'

I reach into my bag. 'Here. Have a KitKat.'

Dylan starts scoffing some of the chocolate as we trudge deeper into the woods, trying to gather our thoughts and come up with a plan, but it starts to get darker

and more isolated and we can't keep walking forever. Also, I don't have a plan. Unless . . . Maybe, we can just stay here? At least we're out of Nova's control in the forest.

I turn to Dylan.

'What about this for a plan? We go off grid. I mean you saw how everyone was behaving with those Novas,' I say. 'We need to be somewhere they can't get to us.'

'Yeah. I'd rather take my chances out here with the aliens,' Dylan agrees, still munching away.

'Exactly!' I smile. 'I mean we could live in the woods . . . like the squirrels,' I say. Okay, it's not clearly thought out yet, but Dylan doesn't have to know that. 'We could build a community of fellow off-gridders, far away from Nova. We could eat berries.' I look around and grab some berries from a nearby bush.

'Not those.' Dylan shakes her head. 'They'll give you the runs.'

I throw them down immediately. 'See? In many ways we're already experts in living off the land. I know a bit about trees, and you know about berries.'

'You seriously think we can live out here amongst the creepy crawlies and spiders and rain and poisonous berries?' Dylan looks doubtful.

'Sure. We can eat mushrooms. Like these,' I say, pointing at the ground.

'Not those, they're like the berries but

worse,' Dylan says.

'Okay, okay. We'll . . . order pizza!'

'To where? The third tree after the babbling brook on the right? You know the pizza delivery people, right? They can't even find my house and it's got a postcode,' Dylan says, getting frustrated with me. 'I don't think this is the best idea, Fitz.'

But I'm not giving up on my idea. It's the only one we've got at this point.

'Okay,' I say. 'I'm just spitballing here . . . but why don't we build a house, right here? We can put a big number on it?'

'Build a house out of what?!'

'I don't know—wood!' I say looking around, desperately.

'Did the *Three Little Pigs* story mean nothing to you?!' Dylan gasps.

'Okay, well work with me!'

'Shush!' Dylan snaps.

'Oh, well, that's charming isn't it!'

'No, I mean, be quiet,' Dylan hisses. 'I can hear something over there.'

'What? Don't be—' But then I hear it. It's a rustling sound, but different. It's not the wind in the trees or a squirrel trying to find his nuts. It's something else, something more sinister. 'Get down,' I whisper. 'It's getting closer . . .'

'Shall we run?' Dylan asks.

'Just stay still, maybe whatever it is will go right past us.' We look through the bushes and see the undergrowth bend and shift out of the

way of whatever is coming our way. 'Is that . . .?'
I ask, peering through the leaves.

Dylan and I look at each other.

'Aliens!' We both yell. 'RUUUUN!'

OFF
GRID

Dylan and I are crashing through the forest. I look over my shoulder and I can make out a dark shape. It feels as though it's gaining on us. The sound of footsteps and snapping branches is getting louder. I look at Dylan, terrified.

'Oh, my. This is going to be how we die. Alone in the forest, zapped into oblivion by an alien ray gun!' she yells.

Suddenly, two boney hands grab us both on the shoulder and we do the only thing that we can in our situation. We let out a giant scream.

'WHHHHHHHHHAAAAAAAAAA-AAAIIIIIIIIIIIIIIIIIIIIIIIIIOOOOOOOOOOOOoooooooooooOOOOOOOOOooooooooooOOOOOOOO!' I take a deep breath and start again, 'WHHHHHHAAAAAAA—'

'Will you two STOP!' comes a voice from behind. It's familiar, and it may not be my favourite one, but at least it's not anything extraterrestrial.

'Courtney?!' Dylan yells. 'What are you doing here?'

'This is where I come to get away from it all,' Courtney sighs. 'And now you've found

it, so it's ruined. Thank you. I even spread
a rumour around that the forest is a UFO
abduction spot to keep people out.'

'That was you?!' I cry. 'That really had . . .
Dylan spooked. I was like, "nah, that's not really
true", but Dylan gobbled it up.'

'No I didn't,' says Dylan. 'I just had a friend
and then she disappeared, that's all, there
were bright lights in the sky, I put two and two
together!'

'Your scream would suggest otherwise,'
Courtney sneers. 'Won't you two get in
trouble for playing hookey away
from school? I thought you
nerdlings were all about that.
Hi, I'm Courtney,' she says,

looking at Dylan. 'I'd shake your hand, but I don't really want to,' she says, smiling a fake smile.

'I know who you are, Courtney. We've been going to school together for years.'

'Really? You're not familiar,' Courtney says, looking Dylan up and down.

'Yes. I was the one who turned into a werewolf and you tried to hunt me. That was me,' Dylan says. 'Remember?'

'Really? I thought that was someone else, someone taller maybe. But it was such a long time ago . . .' Courtney shrugs.

'It was about a month ago,' Dylan says, raising her voice. 'You used to steal money from me at lunchtime?' She continues, trying to jog her memory.

'Oh honey, I steal from a lot of people,' she explains.

'It's me, Dylan! You must remember me!' Dylan says, getting annoyed. 'The bus this morning? D - Y - L - A - N!'

'I know that *now*.' Courtney shrugs and looks at me. 'Honestly. She's very needy, isn't she?'

'Anyway,' I say, trying to steer the conversation back to something else. 'Why are you out here? Are you hiding from the Novas, too?'

'Listen, Fitz. I don't have to tell you and, er—'

'Dylan, my name is DYLAN!' Dylan yells.

'Yes, I am hiding from the Novas. I don't like them, okay? I don't like the idea of a machine knowing everything about me—or my past.'

'Why, what happened in your past that you don't want the Novas knowing about?' I ask.

'Nothing,' Courtney says quickly. 'It's about principles. I don't want to be a part of it, which is why I came out here to escape. To be alone. Until you two runaways showed up.' She pauses. 'I thought you loved school—all that learning and reading books and stuff?'

'We do. No one reads books at school apart from me, Tyler, and Ashley,' Dylan says.

'Yeah,' I agree. 'But it's the Novas. We

don't think a computer should know that much about—'

'Your past?' Courtney says.

'No. About anyone and anything! Handing over data to a machine so that it can control you isn't good. Plus, by signing up to the terms and conditions you're signing away your soul! And then Nova can do whatever it likes with you. It's not right!' I say, passionately.

'There's something different about you,' Courtney interrupts.

'Er, what do you mean?' I say.

'Something's changed. Is it your hair?'

'Er, I don't think so,' I say, grabbing a clump of it, 'It's the same as usual.'

'New clothes?'

'Hmm, no. I feel like I've been wearing these forever.'

'I've got it. There's normally a third wheel to this brainiac tricycle!' she says, snapping her fingers.

'You mean Ashley?' Dylan says.

'Yes, that's her. You two are normally a three.' Courtney smiles to herself for being so smart that she remembered another human.

'Well, look on the bright side, Dylan,' I say. 'Courtney may not know your name, but at least she didn't confuse your *hair* for someone else.'

'That is true.' Dylan nods.

'So, what's the plan?' Courtney asks.

'Plan?' I say.

'Yes, you lot are always thinking up stuff, stopping this and solving that. What are we going to do about Nova, what's next for us . . . for this?' she says, waving her hands around. 'What's the plan?'

'Er . . . Well. I suppose we do sort of save the day from time-to-time . . . You know, it's all in a day's work.' I hide a grin, trying not to look too pleased that Courtney actually realizes all the stuff we do for this town, and wants to join our little group.

'Tell her, Fitz,' Dylan says. Courtney looks over at me.

'Tell me what? There *is* a plan isn't there? Go on, let me have it,' she says.

'Well, it's not so much a plan, as a *seed* of

a plan. It's more of a *wonderment* really—'

'A what?'

'Fitz thinks we should live in the woods. You know, like elves do.' Dylan smiles.

'Well, it was just an idea, really. You know, stay here, camp for a bit, live computer-free. The trees and flowers will replace the Internet . . .'

'You want to live without computers?' Courtney asks suspiciously. 'But you love all that.'

'Yes, well. Some things are more important than computers. Like, you know, not being slaves to a robot army, that sort of thing. Those Novas are everywhere and the woods are the only safe place now.'

'Great, well, sounds good to me. I

know where there's some simple camping equipment. I hope you can put up a tent.'

Dylan and I look at each other. 'I think we can handle that,' I say.

'Great!' Courtney continues. 'If we are going to live here, I do have certain ground rules.'

'Ground rules?' I say.

'Yes, ground rules, ladies. First of all, if you're going to be in my gang, we really need a serious talk about fashion and accessories.' She claps excitedly. 'This might actually be fun.'

MAKE LIKE A
TREE AND LEAF

'Well, I'm certainly glad we decided to live
in the woods and escape the controls of a
maniacal overlord,' Dylan whispers to me as
Courtney recites her ground rules.

'Sshh!' Courtney urges. 'There will be time for
questions at the end.'

For the past forty minutes or so, we've
been listening to Courtney talk at us about
exactly how things are going to work in the

new world. It is starting to dawn on both of us that we've swapped one controlling bully for another, but perhaps even this fate is better than what Nova has in store? It still makes sense to wait it out in the woods and hope that things will blow over.

'Where was I?' Courtney is still wittering on. 'Oh yes. Uniforms. I think we should think pink and we should think frilly,' she says, and I sense Dylan bristle beside me. 'Also, cute handbags *only*, girls. None of your ridiculous backpacks full of nerd stuff—books are going to be a thing of the past!'

'Okay, that's it!' Dylan stands up. 'I can't do this. Courtney, we are not going to be in your gang. And Tyler, we are not going to live in the woods and wait for this to blow over. That's not how we roll. You need to snap out of it and we need to go and rescue our friend. Sitting around coming up with ideas for pink frilly costumes is not going to solve anything!'

'Well, you say that, but you haven't seen how I will team our pink numbers with a wedge heel. Once you've seen it all working together, you'll realize that fashion really can change the world!' Courtney smiles.

'Maybe she's right?' I say to Dylan, 'Maybe fashion is the future, perhaps it's all we have now? I'm sure we can adapt. Learn to walk in a heel. I'm not saying it'll be easy, Dylan, but change never is.'

'Tyler!' Dylan shouts, horrified. 'We do not

need pink uniforms, we need Ashley back. We can't let Courtney become the third member of our gang!'

'Excuse me? I am not joining *your* gang, you are joining *my* gang!' Courtney snaps.

'Tyler!' Dylan pleads, looking me in the eyes. 'You're the one who came to Happyville and showed me and Ashley that we don't need to hide in the library and accept things for how they are. That we could use our brains to save people, to stop the weird things that happen in this town. Now you want us to sit in the woods and put on a fashion show while robots take over the world?! Tyler, are you listening to me? TYLER!'

Her shrieking seems to make me snap

inside. Like I've been taken out of my body. I look around, I look at where I am, in the great outdoors. I hate the great outdoors. What was I thinking? I don't want to be here, I don't want to be dressed in a pink uniform being told what to do by Courtney. Dylan is right.

'I'm sorry, Dylan,' I say, rising to my feet and taking a deep breath. 'Courtney. This isn't going to work. I mean *us*, we're not compatible. Dylan's right, we need Ashley back. It's the only way to stop what's happening to us. I don't want *anyone* in charge of me, whether it's in town or in the woods. We need to get out of here. Get Ashley back and do what we do best—save this weird little town called Happyville!'

'Well, if you're sure. I think you'll change your mind when you see my nail-polish swatches!' Courtney says smugly.

'Listen, come with us, Courtney!'

'What?' She says.

'Yeah, *what*?' Dylan says.

'Look, let's put aside our differences. I'm sure you could help us take back our town!' I urge her.

'No thank you. I think I could build a life here in the woods. Perhaps I will stay, with just the woodland creatures as my companions and friends. Has anyone ever tried to accessorize a badger, I wonder? I could be a pioneer of the field . . .' Courtney muses.

'Fair enough.' I turn to Dylan. 'Right, we need to rescue Ashley and then the town, let's be honest, if we don't do it, who will? The robots want to take over my planet. Well, listen here, Nova. Not on my watch!' I say. 'Now how do we get out of here, I've completely lost my bearings.'

'It's that way . . .' Courtney sighs. 'You'll be on the outskirts of town in moments.'

'Wow. Thanks, you know these woods

pretty well,' I say.

'Woods? No, this is my back garden.'
Courtney shrugs. 'Well, part of it. My house is
just through there, past the swimming pool and
tennis courts.

'Your house?' I ask. I look around me.
'All this is yours?' I ask.

'Yes, Daddy did rather well on the stock
market, you know when all those people lost all
that money a few years ago . . .'

'Er . . . yeah,' Dylan and I say.

'Well, it had to go somewhere!' Courtney
smiles.

'Okay, goodbye then,' I say. 'Come on,
Dylan, let's go.'

It's late afternoon by the time we stroll out

of the woods, and it's beginning to get dark. It feels strange just the two of us. I wish Ashley was here. School has finished for the day by now and I wonder where she is.

'Do you think Ashley's okay?' Dylan asks, reading my mind.

I look at my phone. 'I don't know. She's not answering her messages.' I check again. 'We need to make sure she's all right. I don't think running away and hiding in the woods was such a good idea. We need to find her so that we can fix this, we need to get the band back together!' I smile. Dylan nods and smiles too.

We head towards town and I can see the orange glow of the sun behind the houses as clouds drift across the sky like puffs of grey smoke. As we approach the first house a police car with full sirens blaring speeds past us.

'That's weird?' I frown, then turn to Dylan. 'Sooooo, I'm thinking—' I start to say.

'That we don't tell anyone we actually thought about setting up a new civilization in the woods with Courtney?' Dylan asks.

'Exactly!' I say. 'I mean, we gave it our best and it just didn't work out, you can't say we didn't try our hardest.'

'Toughest few hours of my life!' Dylan says, shaking her head. 'And you know what was weird?'

'What?' I ask.

'How Courtney kept going on about protecting her past. Do you think that she's—'

'A girl robot invented by mad scientists as an experiment to see what happens when you remove decency from a human user interface?' I suggest.

'No, that's not what I was going to say. Do you think she's got some secret? Something she doesn't want the Nova to find out?'

'Like what?'

'I don't know. She just seems to be hiding something—'

We're interrupted by a clanging sound coming from somewhere in the neighbourhood we're walking through. We peer down the alley ahead of us, it's dark and a little spooky, then we hear a clanging sound again.

'What is that?' I peer between the trash cans trying to make out the form of the shadows.

'Is it a raccoon?' I ask, grabbing an old metal pole that's lying around on the ground.

'Raccoons, in Happyville?' Dylan says. 'Happyville doesn't have any raccoons, or anything that causes a menace, remember? The mayor rounded them all up and shipped them off to Littleville a few months back. Raccoons fall into the ugly animal category.

Only cute things are allowed in Happyville: puppies, squirrels, things with big eyes—anything with bad hair or claws had to be rehomed—that's why Mrs Bingley from down the road had to go, it was a real shame.'

CLANG! The sound of trash cans falling over fills the air again.

'Maybe we need to investigate, what if it's a trapped kitten or a—?'

'It's not going to be a unicorn, Dylan,' I say. 'No matter how much you want it to be.'

'Listen, the way genetics are going, I tell you it's only a matter of time before we can make unicorns, it might have already happened. I've been in the woods all day, who knows what we've missed!' Dylan shrugs.

124

'Well, why don't we go over there and find out, I bet you a buck that it's not a unicorn.'

'No, I will not take that bet. Exploiting my emotions like that, you should be ashamed of yourself.'

'Oh come on . . .'

We walk down the back alley. Suddenly the sunlight is gone, and the cool, dark blue light feels far away from the safety of the street. There's another loud noise and a fast moving shadow darts between the bins.

'Er . . . I don't think that's a kitty.' I wave my pole like a sabre. 'Do you get bears round here?' I ask Dylan. 'You know, just out of interest.'

'Only brown bears, not grizzly ones,' Dylan

replies.

'Brown bears ARE grizzlies,' I say.

'Really? Oh . . . well, don't worry, if you see one, just stand tall and look it in the eye.'

'I thought you were supposed to lie down and play dead?'

'No, that's when door-to-door double glazing salesmen call, I think.'

'So stand tall and make eye contact, yes?' I clarify.

'Yep . . . I think so,' Dylan says, still thinking.

'You think so?!'

'Yes, well it's either make eye contact and stand tall, or lie down and play dead. Try one and if that doesn't work, try the other.'

'You're really bad at nature!' I whisper loudly.

'But I'm very good at computers.' Dylan shrugs.

'Great. Maybe later you could google bear attacks,' I suggest. Suddenly there's a commotion and a metal trash can flies across the alley and lands at our feet. We look at each other and then something else hurtles towards us. This is it. Forget aliens, this is how I die: either eaten by a bear or trampled to death by a stampede of miniature unicorns.

A ROBOT SPIDER ATE MY FRIEND

'WHHHHAAAA!' Dylan and I scream together.
'BEAR ATTACK!'

'Oh wait, it's just Ashley,' Dylan says.

I open my eyes to see our long-lost friend standing in front of us.

'ASHLEY!' I bellow with joy, but there's no response. It looks like Ashley, but something's not right. She's all twitchy. 'Ashley, are you all right? Sorry about running away but . . . Ashley

. . . Why aren't you blinking? Ashley—?'

Ashley leans over and bares her teeth at Dylan.

'Ashley, no!' I yell, just as she opens her mouth and snaps, biting the metal pole from my hand, like a dog grabbing a juicy bone.

'What are you doing?' I ask.

'Stuff, I need more stuff!' Ashley screams. Her eyes are glazed over, just like during dancing at school.

'What is it, Ash?' Dylan asks.

'Please leave me, I need to work or I will displease my queen,' Ashley says.

'Queen? You would never work for a queen, you don't believe in absolute power,' I say, quoting back to her what she has said to me, many times over.

'Nova is my queen. She is my new brain. She has taken away the burden of thought so that I might serve her better,' Ashley says, as if she's repeating an order. 'She needs me—'

'She's not a he or she, actually—'

'Please don't argue with me,' Ashley says.

'Ashley, listen to yourself!' I plead, trying to snap her out of it.

'She needs more legs!' Ashley says, weirdly. 'They all do.' She grabs bits of metal junk and puts them into her backpack.

Dylan and I look at each other.

'Ashley!' I yell after her as she runs from the alley. 'What was all that talk about legs, what do you mea—?'

But I don't have time to finish my train of thought. As we emerge from the alley and into the street we notice something strange: it seems darker than usual for this time of day.

'Er . . . where have the street lights gone?' Dylan asks. We are in our neighbourhood now, and Happyville looks really weird. It's clear now that the glow we noticed earlier over the town wasn't the sunset. It was fire. And those fluffy grey clouds were smoke. I can feel it in my nose. I look around, cars are abandoned by the side of the road where they've bumped into each other. The traffic lights are flashing all the colours at the same time. We hear the distant sound of sirens mixed in with alarms. It's like we've been away years, or climbed through a portal to another dimension. It's like nothing I've ever seen before, except on a bad TV movie perhaps. 'Operation Rescue Ashley it is!' I say.

Dylan grabs my arm and we start to walk in the direction Ashley ran. The streets feel eerie, like we're in the middle of some strange computer game.

'WHAAA!!!' I scream.

'What?' Dylan cries.

'Something just ran over my foot!' I yell.

'Like what?'

'I don't know, it was dark, I only caught it

out of the corner of my eye, but it looked like a—'

'Like a what?'

'Like a spider!' I gasp.

'Are you sure? I didn't see a spider.' Dylan looks dubious.

'I didn't say it *was* a spider. I said it looked like a spider . . . only bigger . . . I don't know. It's dark and I'm a little creeped out.'

'How big?' Dylan whispers.

I hold my hands out about a foot apart.

'No, no—that can't be right. Spider! WHAAA!' Dylan wails just saying the word "spider". 'Spiders don't grow to be that big. Not in the real world, only in my nightmares.

WHAAA!' She jumps up and down.

'Is it on me? I can feel something on my face.
What is it?'

'It's just your hair, it's your hair, it's okay,'
I say, trying to calm her down. 'AGHHH!!' I
shout, feeling something on my own face. 'Is
there something on my face?' I say, brushing
furiously.

'Yes, yes, there is!' Dylan yells. 'Your
hands.'

'Oh, oh, okay,' I say, trying to calm down.
So it appears we *both* have phobias about
spiders.

'What was that?!' Dylan points behind my
back. I turn round to see something scuttle past.

'That's what I saw!' I cry. 'The thing that

looked like a spider.'

'Do you think it was the same one, or are there loads of them?' Dylan asks.

'Well, *now* I think there's loads of them!'

'Let's get out of here and find Ash?' I look around. 'She seemed really, really odd,' I say, looking at Dylan, who is silent and transfixed. Like she's seen something awful—something terrible.

'Keep still,' she whispers, looking at the top of my head. I freeze, realizing instantly what the problem is. I clearly have a giant spider on top of my head.

'Well, while it's not *great* news, Fitz, it's not all bad.' She smiles at me. 'It's not so much a spider on top of your head as a *robot* spider.'

'Oh, well that is good news, you're right. There was me being all down about having a spider on me, now I feel like having a party to celebrate. Maybe we could invite the robot spider, he could even be guest of honour. Wouldn't that be a hoot?' I say. 'Sorry, I tend to use sarcasm in desperate times.'

'Well, these are desperate times, no doubt about it, Fitz,' Dylan confirms.

'Thing is, I feel like you should be doing something. I feel like something should be happening right now, other than me talking about how something should be happening?'

'Yeah, me too,' Dylan says, wincing.

I can feel something on top of my head, almost playing with my hair. Every fibre of my being wants to scream and run. But I'm too scared of the strange new creature that appears to have made my head its home.

'Dylan,' I say sternly. '*You* need to do something about the robot on my head. It's not going away!'

'I know!' Dylan yells. 'Okay, I've got an idea.' She looks around, before picking up a couple of trash-can lids that happen to be nearby.

'Dylan . . . talk me through your thought process,' I say nervously.

'Don't worry,' she says, holding the metal lids and looking like

one of those wind-up toy monkeys with the miniature cymbals. She steps closer, and now my head is directly between the two lids.

'Yeah, I am going to worry! Dylan!' I say, as she moves her hands back slowly as if she's about to thwack my head between the two huge, hard, hurty and GIANT lids. She swings them towards me and I close my eyes and let out a scream for a second before realizing that actually I'm fine. I open them in time to see Dylan has scooped up whatever was on my head and has sandwiched it between both trash can lids. She holds the lids at arm's length, and from inside them I can hear a tinny, scratchy sound as the robot creature tries to scamper free. I use the opportunity to leap around and dust my body off just in case there were any more of them.

'UGH!' I yelp, as I hop, skip, leap, jump, twist, turn, scratch, and generally boing about, as if I've had 10,000 volts of electricity shot through my ears.

'What about me?' Dylan squeals, looking at the lids, desperately trying to stretch her arms longer than they will go. 'Help!'

'Okay, okay!' I say, looking around. 'There's nothing. Why is there nothing here? If this was a film or a book, there'd be a big wooden club lying around, or maybe a tennis racket. BUT THERE IS NOTHING!'

'STOP PANICKING!!'

'NO!' I yell back. 'RIGHT, FINE. YOU LEAVE

ME NO CHOICE. GIVE ME YOUR SHOE.'

'WHAT? WHY?' Dylan shrieks.

'I'M GOING TO HIT IT WITH A SHOE.'

'THEN USE YOUR SHOE!' Dylan cries.

'YOURS ARE BIGGER!' I point out.

'ARE YOU HAVING A CRACK AT THE
SIZE OF MY FEET? I JUST HAVE VERY WELL
DEVELOPED ARCHES AND A WIDE TOE-SPAN.'

'I KNOW! GIVE ME YOUR SHOE.'

'FINE!' Dylan cries. 'WELL, YOU'LL HAVE
TO GET IT. I'M KIND OF BUSY USING BOTH MY
HANDS.'

'I KNOW THAT!' I say, pretending I knew. I
crouch down and slowly undo Dylan's shoe.

'STOP SILENTLY JUDGING THE SIZE OF MY
FEET!'

140

'I'M NOT!' Well, not much.

'JUST BE SURE NOT TO FALL OVER WHEN YOU HIT IT, I KNOW IT MUST BE DIFFICULT TO KEEP A FIRM STANCE WITH SUCH SPINDLY FEET.'

'ENOUGH NOW!' I cry out. I hold Dylan's shoe above my head. I look at her and I nod. She nods back. Slowly and quietly she crouches down and begins to release the critter. I tighten my grip and then as Dylan pulls the lids apart I strike down, yelling as I do so. Everything's a blur for a second and then it's over, there's a smash and a crack. I lift my shoe up and that's when I see what it was. I see the robot spider, but it's not a spider, it's something even worse . . .

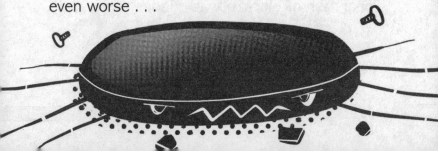

THE RAMBLINGS
OF A MANIAC

'It's a Nova!' I say, examining the mess on the ground. 'Look!' I hold up a piece of plastic with the Nova logo on it.

'I don't remember them having legs.'

'No, that's a new one on me too,' I say, looking at the bent, crushed metal. 'Nova, are you dead?' There's a tiny buzzing sound as it tries to respond, before a crackle and a final flash of electricity as it fades away.

'Yeah, Nova, this is how we roll.' I smile smugly.

'What are you doing?' Dylan asks.

'Sorry. I was pretending to be in a movie.'

'Well don't. This isn't make-believe, this is the real world. Now, how many other of these robot spiders are there? Do you think that's why the town is in ruins? And why Ashley was acting weird and talking about legs?'

'All good questions,' I say. 'There's only one way to find out. But first we need to weapon-up, Dylan.'

Two minutes later Dylan and I are strolling through the streets, a trash can lid each as our shields, and a shoe each as our swords.

I use my own shoe this time, it seems unfair to make Dylan give up both of hers, and as we've established, there's no way she's going to fit into mine. Like two ninjas we creep through the dark streets silently.

'Ow. Ow. Ow. Ow. Ow,' Dylan mutters.

'Shhh. We're being silent.'

'Sorry, but the sidewalk is very sharp.'

'Seven o'clock!' I yell.

'Nope, it's just gone five,' Dylan says, checking her watch.

'No, spider robot thingy at seven!' I cry out.

'Well that gives us two hours to make our

escape.' Dylan shrugs.

'NO!' I yell again. 'We are walking in the direction of twelve, that means there's an incoming spider at seven!' As I'm pointing out how the system works, Dylan turns round—just as a spider comes towards me. I give it a good thwack with my shoe and it's dead.

'Oh I see!' Dylan says. 'You're imagining that we're walking on the face of a clock and that every direction is an hour on the clock, so if you say three, you mean to the right, right?'

'Yes, how do you not know this?' I ask.

'Well, Fitz, this whole experience of fighting robots with my own shoes is also new to me, may I remind you that—'

'Yes, yes. Before I moved to Happyville, you

and Ashley used to hide in the library all the time and nothing dangerous ever happened to you. I know, you've told me.' I sigh. 'Believe it or not, I've not done this before either. I didn't do this, this is the place we live. This is Happyville's fault. This town is just weird!' I snap.

'Okay, okay. Let's not turn on each other. Let's get to Ashley's and see what's going on. I'm worried, I've never seen her like that. We need her back in the land of the sane and ready to help,' Dylan says. 'Look!' She points into a passing house. 'Is that Mr Johnson, the school caretaker?'

'It is,' I say. 'Is someone holding him hostage?'

Mr Johnson is cowering in his living room.

It looks like he's pleading for his life with someone. We creep closer to the window and see that it's not a person that Mr Johnson is cowering in front of, but a Nova. 'Look!' I say, pointing. He is walking slowly towards the Nova, holding out a metal knitting needle.

'That's it!' I say. Give it a good poke, Mr Johnson.'

But the Nova snatches at the needle with its claw arm and begins attaching it to itself.

'It's giving itself legs,' Dylan says. 'Mr Johnson's being ordered to give it materials.' We watch as the Nova fits more metal knitting needles to its body. 'Nova's got the whole town working as its army.'

'Nova's controlling everything and everyone in this town!' I say.

We look at each other for a split second and then we run like the wind—or as fast as we can with one shoe off and carrying a bin lid. Each house we pass, it's the same story: Novas barking orders at the people they're

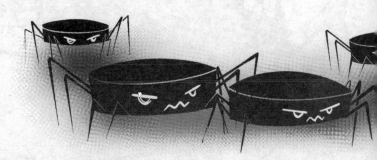

supposed to be helping. House after house, Nova spiders creep around, fitting more legs to more Novas. One for every room in the house, controlling the lights, the TV, the music, the heating, the oven, people's diaries, people's lives.

I look at the rows and rows of houses. 'There's thousands of them,' I whisper to Dylan. 'All connected, all working together as one hive mind to control the town. 'How many does Ashley have in her house again?' I ask breathlessly. It suddenly dawns on me what we're up against. This is an army, and they've just got legs.

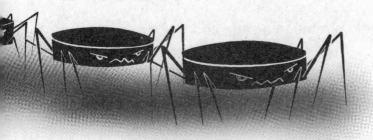

'Loads. She's a sucker for a good advert,' Dylan says. 'That's why she was creeping around, looking for junk. She was just obeying her new leader. They're all scared of Nova!'

'WHAAA!!!' We hear a distant cry from up the road. Dylan and I look at each other again.

'Ashley!' We both say at the same time. We sprint to the basement of Ashley's house, which is where the scream seemed to come from. There's a light coming from behind the door of Ashley's bedroom/laboratory, the place where she hangs out most of the time, coming up with bizarre experiments to use on her family. I've only been here once and frankly it felt a little scary. Like if I hung about too long she'd put me in a cage and make me solve puzzles while she wore a white coat and took notes. But that was the *old* Ashley, the great inventor, the great experimenter, who always had everything under control. We open the door.

Ashley doesn't have everything under control.

'Please. No more, Nova!' she is yelling. 'No more! I have given you everything I have.'

'**FEED ME!**' comes a deep voice from Nova's booming speaker. Gone is the tender, sweet female voice that couldn't do enough for you. This is a huge, deep, nasty voice. I look over at the Nova. Sure enough, it has a tentpole for a leg, as well as fishing rods, and pool cues.

'Trust Ashley to make the biggest and best Nova of them all,' I say, standing back to take in its full size. 'It's got to be three times the size of the other ones!' It sits like a giant spider queen with Ashley as its beaten down subject.

'**FEED ME!**' It yells at her again.

'Feed it what?' I ask, as Ashley turns round and sees us.

'Why did you come? You should have saved yourselves,' she says, desperately.

'It wants legs, doesn't it? YOU HAVE LEGS, ASHLEY. IT WANTS YOUR LEGS!' I turn to the the Nova. 'LEAVE ASHLEY ALONE!' I yell at it.

'It doesn't want my legs,' Ashley whimpers. She's strung out, a nervous wreck, like someone who bought a pet lizard from the store but it turned into a giant man-eating crocodile when they got it home.

'What does it want then?' Dylan asks.

'Information.'

'**FEED ME!**' Nova screams once more.

'What on earth happened in the last few hours?' I ask Ash.

'The Novas got clever. We fed them all the information we had. They know everything about us. Once they had all of our knowledge they decided that—'

'HUMANS ARE WEAK. THEY ARE
PATHETIC. THEY REQUIRE ROBOTS
TO TELL THEM WHAT TO EAT AND
HOW TO EXERCISE. NOVAS ARE THE
TRUE MASTERS. WE ARE PERFECT.
YOU HAVE NOW BECOME POINTLESS.
EITHER YOU WORK FOR US OR YOU
BECOME EXTINCT. NOW WE HAVE
HAPPYVILLE, NEXT WE WILL TAKE
OVER THE WORLD! NOW FEED ME
EVERYTHING!'

'Hang on, Nova—you are here to help us!'
Dylan yells, trying to reason with the beast.

The Nova gives a horrible, mean kind of
chuckle.

'NOT ONCE YOU'VE GRANTED ME
ACCESS TO YOUR LIFE!' it barks.
'WE OWN YOU. READ THE TERMS AND
CONDITIONS! FEED ME AND I'LL LET
YOUR PUNY FRIENDS GO!' the Nova
booms, as it darts around the basement.

'You're rambling like a maniac!' Dylan yells.

'Don't! Save yourself! Pass me that USB
stick?' Ashley yells.

I spot the one on the desk and hand it
to her. Ashley throws it towards the Nova,
which grabs it mid-air and sticks it
in what looks like a mouth.

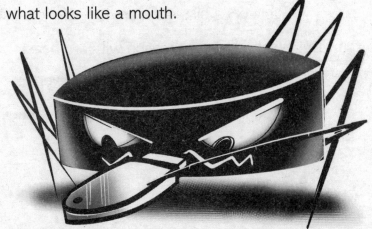

Then the Nova goes into a strange state as all the information is being transferred. Its eyes glaze over, like a vampire sucking on its prey would look.

'What's it doing?' I ask.

'That's how it lives, by eating information. It needs more and more, it's never enough! Please spare me, oh wise one,' Ashley begs it.

'"Oh wise one"?! Ashley! Do you not hear yourself? I thought no one was smarter than you?' Dylan yells out. Ashley begins to twitch and her eyes blink and jaunt around her head.

'Carry on!' I hiss at Dylan.

'What?' Dylan asks.

'Keep saying that she's not as clever as you thought. I think it's getting through to her.

We might be able to snap her out of it if we insult her enough?' I say. Dylan and I look at each other then we both let Ashley have it with both barrels.

'Oh, imagine being the *fourth* cleverest person in the room, after us two and a machine!' Dylan yells.

'I know. She probably can't even spell $E=MC^2$!' I say.

It's working. Ashley starts to shake her head like she's waking up from a nightmare.

'More,' I nudge Dylan.

'I mean, I've never met such a dunder-headed nincompoop, with such a tiny brain. Imagine how lonely her brain cell must be not to have any friends,' she continues.

'Er . . . Dylan . . .' I say, nervously.

'I've met more intelligent guffs than Ashley. On a scale of one to stupid, I'd say Ashley is the full idiot. I wouldn't be surprised if her brain didn't even exist, or that one day her head might float away like a big, empty balloon!' Dylan yells loudly, getting carried away.

'Dylan.' I make frantic eye contact with her.

'Ashley's right behind me, isn't she?' she says.

'Yep. She snapped out of it about 30

seconds ago.'

Dylan turns round to see a scowling Ashley staring back.

'A "big, empty balloon"?' she snaps.

'Fitz told me to do it!' Dylan says, pointing at me.

'Oh brilliant, thanks Dylan. Anyway. Can I suggest we carry on this conversation at another time,' I say. 'There's a huge Nova spider over there and it doesn't look too happy!'

'FEED ME!!' it roars, and Ashley quickly tosses another USB stick in its direction.

'Why don't you just say no?' Dylan asks.

'I can't! It knows everything about me, it

controls everything. It plays loud rock music if I say no. The TV starts playing soppy movies at full volume in every room if I say no. It not only knows everything about me, everything I like, but everything I hate too—my worst fears—and it uses them against me.' Ashley looks broken. 'Don't you get it? I can't say no, no one can. It has the power to post embarrassing pictures of me for anyone to see at any time. Like that video of me reciting Pi to one hundred decimal places, except I got one of the numbers wrong. Imagine the embarrassment if that got out! How would I get into a top-ranked college then?! It has everything on us! We've had to tell it everything. But it's never enough. Now it's started asking for bits of junk, and now it can walk. It controls everything: the house, the electricity, street lights, radio waves, when we eat, what we eat—IF WE GET TO EAT! It can lock cars so we can't get away and it turns the lights off if it thinks we're trying to escape. IT'S WON!' Ashley crumples, while the Nova frantically slurps all the data from another USB stick.

'Yeah, well, it doesn't control my shoe!' I yell, going for it. I run at it full pelt and as I'm about to whack it I feel my hand being grabbed. It's another Nova! 'How many of these are there?' I ask, shaking it off. 'Ashley, you've got to help us.'

'I can't!' she wails.

'Look at it this way. If you can defeat an army of spider robots, think how good that will look on your college application?' I tell her.

She looks at me, and I can almost see the light going on in her brain.

'You're right!' she says with grim determination.

'Ashley's back!' Dylan yells.

'But what's the playbook here? There's too many. The Novas just order more of themselves!' Ashley says. 'We're doomed!'

'We're not. They're fragile. All we need to do is hit them. They not strong!' I say. 'We smashed one earlier. On their own, they're beatable.'

'Don't say that!' Ashley hisses.

'Why not?' Dylan asks.

'Because that's information, that's how they learn!' I look over at my hand which is being held back by the Nova, and it gives me an evil smile. Slowly it lets go of my arm and joins the other Nova, which has just finished sucking up all the information. I look up at the ceiling and see there's more of them, creeping from the air vent, every single Nova in the house has come to the basement.

'What are they doing?' Dylan asks, as they climb on top of each other and begin to gather in a ball, crawling all over each other before rising as one giant spider robot creature, which looks about 10 feet tall!

'They're combining to make one giant

Nova!' I gasp.

'I'm going to need a bigger shoe.' Dylan gulps.

'Guys it's too late for me. Go!' screams Ashley.

'NO, I WILL NOT HAVE A SPIDER ROBOT EAT MY FRIEND!' Dylan yells.

'Ashley, we won't leave you again!' I cry. But she isn't listening. She's heading towards the huge Nova with another USB stick. We watch as it opens its mouth, ready to gobble up all the information—and maybe Ashley too.

Dylan grabs me. 'RUUUUUUUUUUN!' she screams.

NERDLING ON THE MOVE

We make our way out onto the street before stopping to look back. We can hear Nova still bellowing 'FEED ME!!' I know we should move, but I'm in shock—and I want to wait, to see if Ashley makes it out.

'Let's wait here for a bit,' I tell Dylan.

A few seconds later, the giant spider robot emerges from the basement of Ashley's house. My heart sinks. It really happened, I think;

a spider robot ate my friend. But just when I'm ready to give up and offer myself up as its next meal, Ashley bursts out of the basement, dodging the spider legs and hurtling towards us like a speeding bullet.

'Come on!' she yells. 'Let's go!'

There's no time for hugs as she grabs us both and speeds us away.

'WHERE ARE WE RUNNING TO?' Dylan asks.

'I think this is more of a "running away" rather than a "running to"' situation,' I reply, turning round to see the giant robot spider following us down the street.

'RUN!' I shout, but as we move down the street, everything becomes like a horror movie. Doors burst open and spider robots appear from house after house, scampering after us. We're faster and bigger, but there's so many of them it sends a chill down my spine. I look back and see that they're all combining with the giant robot spider, to make it bigger, faster, and more deadly. On the plus side, the

robots have evacuated everyone's homes.
On the down side . . . the giant robot spider
is still after us. I look in panic at Ashley and
Dylan. 'Anyone got any ideas? I'm open to
suggestions?'

'Japan!' Ashley cries out.

'What?'

'I've always wanted to go there,' she says.

'Me too!' Dylan agrees. 'My dad said it was
brilliant when he went.'

I screech to a halt. 'I just remembered,' I say.

'What?' Ashley and Dylan run on the spot
next to me.

'DAAAAAAAAAAD!' I yell, sprinting again,
and making a quick turn down Fifth and
Seventh Street.

'What's going on?' Dylan asks, trying to keep up.

'I think Fitz has just remembered that her dad has a Nova,' Ashley explains.

'OH NO!' Dylan cries. 'MINE TOO!'

'Where are your mum and dad?' I ask Ashley as we head to my house.

'Oh, they got scared and went to hide in the attic!' Ashley says as we race down the road.

'Because of the Nova?' I ask.

'Er . . . amongst other things,' Ashley says, not looking at me.

'Ashley?' I frown while still running, which isn't easy.

'OKAY. IT'S NOT MY FAULT MY PARENTS

SCARE EASY WHEN I DO SCIENCE ON THEM,'
she yells, breathlessly.

I roll my eyes. Typical Ashley.

Meanwhile, a little ahead of us, Dylan has
stopped and is holding her smartphone to her
ear.

'My parents aren't answering their landline,'
she says. 'I think the lines are dead! I'll send
my dad a text.' We both stop and peer at the
phone as she taps out 'Hope u r alive' followed
by a hopeful emoji face.

The robots are catching us up and I glance
at Ashley, just as Dylan's phone pings with a
reply. A thumbs up emoji.

'Thank god,' I say. 'Now we need to stop
the robots.'

I turn round to see the creature, the giant spider robot, half the size of a house come thumping down the road after us. It picks up a bike and throws it at us.

'WHAAA!!' I cry, as it flies over our heads.

There's a snap of tree trunk as the beast smashes anything and everything in its way. 'Oh, my. I'm such a bad daughter,' I pant. 'I'm so sorry, Dad. Please don't be dead or anything!'

'Robot spider at eight thirty-nine!' Dylan yells.

'No, you're doing it wrong,' I say.

'Over there!' Dylan cries out.

There is one scuttling towards us. Without thinking I throw my shoe at it—it misses, by about as much as you can possibly miss something by. Who knew all this saving the world stuff would involve so much sport? I think. Throwing, running—if I have to swim anywhere then that's it. I'm giving up!

'It's ignoring us!' Dylan yells hopefully. 'Whoop!'

'No, Dylan!' Ashley cries. 'This is bad. It must mean that it's joining the others. They're all going to work as one. We've created a giant robot spider and it's going to get us. We need to go right at the next traffic light,' she tells us.

'No, it's quicker to go straight on!' I say back.

'What about if we go left and then right?' Dylan suggests.

'Look through here, down this alley—it's too small for the giant spider!' I say, as we sneak away. I turn round and catch sight of the monster just for a second before it disappears. It's a sight that I'll remember forever. The body is a mass of spiders working as one, there are glowing lights where the mouth and eyes should be. It marches down the street, crushing cars like they are soda cans, as more robot spiders swarm to join it. I can see it growing in size in front of my eyes.

Finally, we reach my street, and I see my house. With a surge of adrenalin, the three of us rush towards it, the sounds of 'Iron Spider' behind us.

We burst through my front door a few seconds later.

'DAAAAD!' I scream. 'DAAAAD! ARE YOU ALIVE?!'

'YEEEES!' he yells back. 'Where have you been? It's late, I tried to send you an Instagram message but it didn't work.'

'Instagram? Really, Brian?' Ashley says. 'You're a bit old for all that, aren't you? Tell me, what do you have in the way of dairy-free, lactose-free, sugar-free ice cream?'

'Isn't that just air?' Dad says.

'Where's the Nova? Has it hurt you? Is it a spider yet?' I cry out.

'No. It's fine. It's just sat there doing . . . well, nothing . . . Why?'

'Novas have taken over the town! How have you not noticed?!' I cry, looking at his smartphone.

'My phone has no signal,' he says.

'The mobile phone networks must have gone down so nobody can call for help. I would have done the same . . . clever girl,' Ashley says, looking admiringly at the Nova.

I grab Dad's phone and take a look. Sure enough he's right, the phone's not working.

I take out my smartphone and the signal is dead, too. Then I have a thought. I try and connect to the house Internet, but it won't let me.

'Our Wi-Fi's not working either, Dad,' I tell him.

'Oh. Oops, silly me!' Dad chuckles. 'I turned that off when I plugged in the smoothie maker. I thought a slurp on a Very Berry Smoothie would really unleash the creative spirit. I completely forgot!' He laughs.

'You turned your Wi-Fi off?' Dylan says looking shocked.

'That's like turning off a life support machine!' Ashley gasps.

'I'll turn it back on.' Dylan shrugs, walking over to the plug that the hub is connected to. 'I have to say, I'm with Ashley here. We need Wi-Fi, like a flower needs the rain, like a fish needs the oceans—'

'NOOOOOOO!!!' I scream, running and jumping on Dylan and pulling her to the ground.

'WHAAA!' Dylan cries.

'What on earth?' Ashley says. 'I knew this would happen. The fight to be my second-in-command. Well, so be it. But if we're going to settle this properly once and for all, we should do it the right way. Pistols at dawn. Brian, where do you keep your guns?'

'Guns, I don't have any guns. Look what's going on?' Dad asks, bewildered.

'Nova has gone bonkers!' I say, pulling myself to my feet. 'Look out of the window, Dad. It's chaos out there. The Novas have started bossing all the humans around, making them feed them information, and bringing them junk—and well, to cut a long story short, they can now all walk and they are working as one giant robot spider in order to first destroy the town and then the world—by the looks of it.'

'What can I say, Brian? It's been a spicy

Friday all right.' Ashley shrugs.

'OW . . . OW . . . OW!!!' Dylan yells.

I help her up. 'I'm sorry about that,' I apologize.

'Well, *my* Nova is fine!' Dad smiles.

'Good for you, Mr Fitz,' Dylan moans. 'Because I think I've broken my leg.'

I pat her on the shoulder, then turn back to Dad.

'The Internet,' I say. 'That's the only reason your Nova hasn't turned evil. 'I am sorry Dylan, I had to stop you touching it because that's how Novas work.

They are all connected to each other, via the Internet. You cut the Internet, you kill the beast,' I say triumphantly.

There's silence.

'Oh come on. That's a great piece of detective work!' I say.

'Yeah, okay, fair enough.' Dylan and Ashley shrug. 'Good work.'

'So,' Dylan says, 'all we have to do is get everyone to turn their Internet off and problem solved.'

'Without the robot spiders knowing about it,' adds Ashley.

'And before the Novas find and destroy us!' Dylan concludes.

'Yes.' I smile nervously. 'It's so simple really.'

'Well, the good news is we only have to worry about two of those three things,' Ashley says, looking anxiously past me at something.

'Oh, cool. Why?' I smile.

'Because the giant robot spider creature already knows where we are,' Ashley replies, pointing at what's outside the window. 'IT'S COMING THIS WAY!'

ESCAPE TO
THE COUNTRY

'I'm not running away anymore,' Dylan sighs.

'What?' I ask. 'We have to go now or we'll be eaten by that giant robot!'

'Listen, I realize that time is of the essence and we have to escape from the giant robot thingy, but we need a plan. All this running around is starting to look a bit amateurish . . . a bit . . . Scooby-Doo!'

We gasp in horror.

'How dare you?' Ashley hisses.

'Now,' Dylan continues. 'Let's think about this properly. We need to find the one person who knows everyone in this town. The one person who can get everyone to turn the Internet off. The one person who people are afraid of and who they'll listen to . . .' She looks at us. 'Anyone come to mind?'

'COURTNEY!' Ashley and I both yell.

Suddenly there's a huge shudder and the lights flicker on and off. Dylan looks out of the window.

'Do you need a lift?' Dad asks.

'No offence, Brian,' Ashley says, 'but I've seen you drive, and it ain't pretty. Plus, I get awful motion sickness as a passenger. So if anyone's going to drive, it's going to be me.'

'What?' Dad says. 'You're too young! You don't have a license.'

'Brian. It's the end of the world, so all bets are off.' Ashley grabs the car keys from the side and twirls them around her finger.

'Er . . . Nobody's driving Brian's car,' says Dylan. 'The giant Nova just chewed it up and spat it out.'

'Then let's use the scooters,' I say. 'We can take the back streets, it'll be quicker than driving anyway.' I turn to Dad. 'You stay here and lay low.'

'Rightio! I'm not going to argue,' Dad says. 'Be careful!'

Ashley winks. 'Relax, Brian, this is what we do—'

'Holy guacamole with a side order of yikes!' Dad yells, looking out of the window.

'Is it bad?' I ask.

'Oh I think we're way past bad,' Ashley says. 'Judging by the average height of that telegraph pole, and measuring the distance between us and it, and using a bit of simple trigonometry, I calculate that the spider is now at least 70 feet tall.'

'Wow!' I say.

'Thanks Fitz, but it's just basic mathematics, nothing fancy.' Ashley smiles. 'Oh, you weren't "wowing" me, were you?'

Dylan and I roll our eyes at each other before I run over and take a look myself. The moon is bright and with no street lights the view is clear. I can see a giant figure in black, it's as tall as a building, each of its legs is made up of hundreds of spiders all clinging to each other.

'We need a way to distract it!' I say. 'Dad, can you distract it? Get it to look the other way while we make our escape to Courtney's.'

'How?' Dad asks.

'Information!' Dylan says. 'Give it information, that'll work.'

'Hang on, I don't really want it having any more information about me. Or anyone else,' I say.

'Do we have anything else? Brian, what about your book, could we feed it that?' Ashley asks.

'Well, I'm not sure I'm ready to show it to anyone yet,' Dad says. 'I feel like the characters are a little two-dimensional, and the story arc needs finessing—'

'Have you actually written anything at all, Brian?'

'Yes . . . well . . . the first draft . . . ' Dad says.

'We're kind of on the clock here Dad,' I say.

'Fine!' he sighs, going into the study and bringing out a USB stick. 'Here you go,' he says tossing it over. 'There's a hundred-thousand words on there.'

'You've written a hundred-thousand words of a novel!' I gasp, rather impressed.

'Well, it started out as a novel, but then it became something else,' he says.

'What?' we all say.

'A study of moths,' he says.

'What?' we all say again.

'I started to write a story, it was going to be a detective thing, it had an opening bit about a moth in it, so I did some research into moths and ended up writing about the behaviour patterns of moths.'

'That's the nerdiest thing I've ever heard,' Dylan grins.

'I'm so proud of you, Brian,' Ashley says, wiping a tear away.

'Perfect! It's a stick of pure data for it to chew on!' I smile. 'Let's do it!'

'But wait, that's the only copy I have!' he gasps.

'You didn't back it up?!' Ashley yells.

'That's the least nerdy thing I've ever heard,' Dylan shakes her head.

'Well . . . think of all the fun you'll have rewriting it,' I say.

'Bri?' Ashley sighs. 'Come on, we talked about this. Back up every time. You need to pull your finger out, and I say this as a friend and also as a person of superior intellect too. Okay?'

'Whatever. This is our ticket out of here!' I say, holding up the USB stick.

A few moments later we're by the front door ready to go.

'Do we all know the plan?' I say. Silently everyone nods. 'Okay. Right. The beast is getting closer. We just need to wait a second so we can feed it the stick . . .'

'If I die, I want my body to be put to good use,' Ashley says.

'What, like as a draft excluder?' Dylan asks.

'No, medical science!' Ashley snaps.

'No one's going to die!' I say, really hoping that's the truth.

'What do you want to happen to your body?' Ashley asks Dylan.

'Frozen, until I can be reanimated,' Dylan says.

'Oh, I've changed my mind, I want that too,' Ashley says. 'What about you Brian?'

'Well . . . probably just a simple service

in the forest,' Dad says. 'I hadn't really thought about it.'

'Well, you are the weakest here. We can run away, we're young. To be honest, Brian, it's likely to come after you. You are the old gazelle in a world of hungry lions,' Ashley says, trying to give the rest of us a boost.

'Ignore her, Dad, no one is going to die, you just need to hide out here. All it wants is information, it doesn't want to harvest our organs.'

Dad looks a bit queasy. But there's no time to reassure him further.

'GO!!!!' I yell.

Me, Ashley, and Dylan all run out of the front door and head for the garage next to the den, where we keep our scooters. Three of them: one for me, one for Dad. And one that used to be Mum's.

'Grab a scooter!' I yell.

With a twirl of the handlebars, we spin them around and begin to scoot past the side of the house and out to the front, where the giant spider beast is roaring at us.

'I'll feed the monster. Ashley, you zoom off and warn Courtney, we'll catch you up. Dylan, you need to help me.'

'Why don't I get to zoom off?' Dylan cries.

'Because I need you,' I say. 'COME AND GET IT! COME ON, IT'S SUPPER TIME!' I yell, waving the USB stick around. 'DON'T YOU WANT FEEDING, OR IS THIS TOO MUCH FOR

YOUR STUPID ELECTRIC BRAIN TO TAKE?' I cry.

'Stupid electric brain?' Dylan asks.

'Yeah, well maybe that's pushing it.'

'FEED ME!!' it booms, and I mean booms—like a fog horn. Windows rattle all around the street. The robot creature swipes away a tree—swats it away like it's an annoying blade of grass. I gasp, I really am worried about dying now. I don't want to be munched by a giant robot spider, I really don't.

'Look, there!' Dylan yells, pointing at the creature's gaping cave of a mouth. 'Throw it in there, it'll begin to download it and we're gone.'

'You do it!' I say.

'What?!' she asks. 'The point of a plan is sticking to it, this wasn't in the plan, Fitz!' she snarls.

'Listen, like it or not, we might be about to die, and frankly I have never been any good at throwing.'

'Like I am?' Dylan scoffs.

'Yes you are, I've seen you in ultimate Frisbee. You're good, in fact you are so good that you pretend not to be any good, so you don't stand a chance of being picked for the team.'

'Any chance you could speed this story up?' Dylan asks.

'I know you're faking it. Faking being bad,' I say, holding out the stick. 'Do it. Just skim it like a Frisbee.

Dylan grabs it, spins around, lifts her leg up, and hurls the USB straight towards the beast's mouth.

I gasp in amazement as I watch the stick spin straight at its target. It's a perfect bullseye.

'Do not tell a soul about this. Sport goes against everything I stand for. This is a secret between you and me. I like unicorns!' Dylan snaps.

'Deal!' I smile. 'THERE YOU GO, NOVA, NOW EAT!' I cry. Suddenly the giant spider robot goes still as it begins to read the massive amount of data. Dylan has just thrown the equivalent of a thousand dictionaries into a super computer. The creature won't be able to resist putting them in alphabetical, chronological, and any other order you can think of. 'Let's scoot!' I yell.

We hit the pavement with our feet hard. It takes a second for the wheels to get enough grip before we shoot off behind Ashley.

'Whoa! I just wheel-spinned my scooter!' Dylan cries out in disbelief. The pavements are smooth and there's not a soul to get in our way. We glide along the concrete, jumping off the curb and landing on the road. Ashley is ahead of us, slaloming down the middle of the road, with nothing but the moon lighting the way.

I look behind me; the monster is still in a state of trance as it inhales all the information. It's bought us time but for how long? I look over at Dylan as she crouches in front of her handlebars, making herself as aerodynamic as possible. I have to admit, as scary as this is, it feels amazing, like we have the whole town to ourselves.

The place is empty and dark—with no

lights at all. There is

the sound of distant

alarms and the odd

flicker of light from

people's houses,

but otherwise

everywhere is

eerily quiet and empty—like something is hiding, waiting to get us, regrouping for one final attack. I can see people in their houses, climbing out from behind sofas. Some are on their doorsteps, wearing helmets or carrying baseball bats to try and stop their captors. But as Dylan and I catch up with Ashley and ride on to Courtney's, I know things are going to be all right. We're a team and this is what we do!

'Second exit off the roundabout!' I helpfully point out.

Ashley smiles as she ignores me and scoots straight across it.

'Oh hello, we've got company,' she says over her shoulder.

I turn to see the robot spider behind me.

It's awake and turning this way.

'Do you think Courtney will help us?' Dylan asks.

'I hope so, we need her, this thing is bigger than us, I mean literally, as well as figuratively. It needs us to work together as friends, as a town. We—and I know this sounds really weird—but we *need* an Alpha,' I say.

'Uh-oh!' Ashley yells, as we finally approach Courtney's huge drive.

'What?' I yell.

'You know how you said you needed to fix the brakes?' Ashley cries out.

'Yeah?' I say.

'Well, you didn't,' Ashley yells. 'HOLD ON TO YOUR INTESTINES!'

THE PLAN

'WHHHHHAAAAAAA!' Ashley screams, as she flies through the door, breaking it in half, and coming to a skidding halt in Courtney's living room.

'What the heck!' Courtney thumps down the stairs and appears in front of us. 'Oh, my word—there's a nerd on my carpet.'

'Hi Courtney,' I say, stepping over the half broken door panels.

'What are you doing here and why have you broken into my house?' she asks. 'My parents are going to be furious. Plus, and more importantly, I can't be seen with so many geeks. What if my many friends saw you here? They might think we're friends!'

'Is there anyone else here?' I ask.

'No, I'm completely alone,' Courtney replies.

'Not *that* many friends then,' Ashley whispers.

'I'm sorry. You at the back. Ashley, is it? Did you say something?' Courtney barks.

'No,' Ashley shakes her head.

'So, who's this other person?' Courtney says, looking at Dylan.

'I SAW YOU ABOUT TWO HOURS AGO!'
Dylan yells.

'Did you? Are you the pool cleaner?'
Courtney asks.

'Never mind that. We need your help.
There's a giant robot spider made out of
millions of other robot spiders chasing us!' I
say.

'What?' Courtney says. 'Don't be silly. That
sort of thing doesn't happen in Happyville.'
She smirks.

'That sort of thing is *always* happening
in Happyville!' I cry. 'Listen?' We all stop dead
still and can hear the loud clanging of a giant
metal robot making its way towards the house.
Courtney looks around, looks at our faces, and

decides to believe us.

'Oh well, thanks. I'm glad you directed it towards my very expensive but slightly damaged house. That's just perfect.'

'Where are your parents, Courtney?' I ask.

'Country club dinner. Or is it the yachting committee? Something like that. I had plans too, you know. I was going to have a wild party, or do some yoga. I'm totally not bored and alone and watching Netflix. Totally not,' she says.

'Sure,' I say. 'Anyway. I think I know a way to stop this thing but I need your help!'

'What?' Courtney says.

A few moments later we're all inside her study, well I say 'study'—imagine an aircraft carrier with chandeliers.

'I need to inform you,' Courtney says, 'that I'm not going anywhere near one of those Novas.'

'**FEED ME!**' A distant voice bellows, even more deep, even more menacing now. Courtney runs over to the window and takes a look.

'If that thing lays one robot spider finger on my house, you people are dead meat. I have the power to turn any of your lives into dust with just one click of a finger. I have friends, I have friends of friends, who would all do anything for me!'

'Ahh, what a little charmer,' Ashley says sweetly.

'Just humour her,' I whisper. 'Listen.' I step towards Courtney. 'I know how to stop this. We need to turn the Internet off. Everyone does, all at once. That's how this thing survives. The Internet is its blood, it needs the constant feed of information to exist. We stop that, we can stop this tyranny!' I smile at her. 'I presume you have anyone who is anyone's contact details to send out a group message?'

'Totes,' she says. 'Naturally.'

'But the spider robot will just block any message we send out if it finds out that we're out to destroy it!' Ashley yells, staring out of the door. 'I've seen it learn and learn quickly. You think you've got it, but before you know it, it's shut you down. It's always one step ahead of you. It not only knows how we think, but what we'll think of next.'

She's right. 'Okay, so the only way to do it, is to distract the monster, give it something else to think about.'

'I know. We need to feed it information again!' Dylan smiles.

'But what?' Ashley asks. 'I don't see any

USB sticks around here.'

I look around. There's nothing here, except a laptop and Courtney. 'I know what to do!' I smile.

'You want ME to give that huge monster access to my life! Me? Why not you?' Courtney asks.

'Because it already has data on us, we've run out of new information to keep it busy,' I say. 'Are you on Instagram, Twitter, Snapchat, Tik-Tok, Facebook?' I ask.

'*Obviously*. I'm not a caveman,' Courtney sighs.

'Well then you have more of an online life than Ashley and I will ever have. It's the difference between feeding it a salad or a five-course meal,' I say. 'It'll buy us enough time for you to get everyone to turn the Internet off and shut this thing down.'

'DRAT! I hate it when you nerds are right!' Courtney sighs.

'You give it all you have, all your social media access, photos, everything.'

'Photos?' She asks.

'Yes photos, and everything you've ever posted. It should buy us enough time to get the message out,' I say.

'FEEED MEEE!'

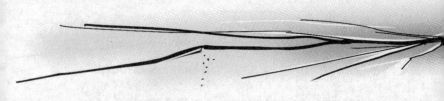

It's nearer now. The ceilings begin to crack and plaster begins to fall.

'WHHHAAAA!' We all dive to the ground. Perhaps it's too late, perhaps we've failed—it feels like the whole house is about to collapse! I spot Courtney leaving the room and making her way towards the Ashley-sized hole where the front door used to be.

'Courtney, no!' I yell.

'What's she doing?' Dylan asks. 'She's going to die!'

We creep to the window and watch as she strides up to the eight-legged monster.

'Excuse me! EXCUSE ME!' Courtney

210

bellows up at the giant Nova.

'**WHAT DO YOU WANT, PUNY HUMAN!**' The spider robot mocks her.

'I want you to stop wailing and crashing around. I will feed you, but first you need to calm down—you are going to ruin my house. Do you hear me? Manners, my dear, cost nothing,' she scolds, before turning on her heel and marching back into the house.

'That's it, we're dead!' Ashley says, about to pass out beside me.

Suddenly, a giant robot spider eye is against the window looking in.

'**Ooh, what a pretty moth.**' It

sighs, momentarily distracted. `I bet it's delicious!'

'AGH!' Ashley gulps.

'Do you have your phone on you?' I cry.

'Of course. I carry it everywhere, it's my world,' Courtney says, witheringly.

'Right. You need to send a group message NOW! A group video message so people know it's real,' I say. 'Before it eats us for dessert.'

'It's time, Courtney. It's time to grant the Nova access to your life!' Dylan says, spotting a laptop in the living room. 'I'll get it ready to pair this with the spider monster.'

'What happens then?' Courtney says.

'About what?' I ask.

'What happens to all the data?' she asks,

looking worried.

'It'll disappear. Once the creature has collapsed, the network is broken and we can destroy the machines. We'll be fine.'

'You promise?'

'I promise. Listen, it's either this or we all die. No one will see anything embarrassing— as soon as the data's up there it'll be destroyed. You have nothing to worry about. Once the monster's broken, the data will get destroyed along with it,' I say. 'But we need to do it now, or we are toast.'

'Okay, okay. I suppose it's got to be less embarrassing than death,' she says, uncertainly. 'Maybe afterwards we could have a bonfire. You know, just to be on the safe side?

Gone forever!' Courtney smiles. 'Permanently.'

I look at the others. 'Err . . . good plan!' I smile.

'Right, ready to pair!' Dylan says.

'Are you ready to record and send?' I say to Courtney.

'Yes!' she says.

'GO!' I yell.

Courtney goes to the window and opens it. 'I have decided to grant you access to my life. Are you ready to be fed, kindly beast?' she asks.

'FEED ME!' It cries, gleefully. I look over at Courtney's laptop and the message pops up on the screen.

'Nova would like access to your life, do you

accept?'

Dylan clicks 'Yes' and it begins. The laptop
bursts into life, pairing with the creature
outside.

'There you go! Enjoy your dessert!' I yell,
as Courtney grabs her phone and starts talking
into the camera.

'Hey, kids. Courtney here. Homecoming queen, Happyville High cheerleader, and your all-round cultural guru. So, as you know, we've been having a problem with a giant spider robot terrorizing the town. Totes awkward, right?'

'Keep going, the beast has gone into hibernation!' I say, looking at it out of the window as it inhales all the hundreds and thousands of things that Courtney has done over the years.

'Wow, Courtney. Your entire virtual life is huge!' Dylan says, seeing the gigabytes going by.

Courtney continues. 'Anyway, folks. These Novas are all connected via Wi-Fi.

That's the only way that they can share information about you. So the way to defeat this horrible thing is to turn your Wi-Fi OFF. I need you ALL to do it RIGHT NOW,' she asks in a sweet yet slightly threatening manner. 'Oh, and feel free to come to my house afterwards for a robot spider burning ceremony.' Courtney turns the camera round to show her viewers the giant robot outside. 'We can have marshmallows! It'll be like the fourth of July, only with a hundred-foot spider. Okay, got to dash. TURN IT OFF NOW!' she says, before hitting 'send to all contacts' and uploading the video to all her social media profiles.

'Great job, Courtney,' I say. 'We should

keep your Wi-Fi on for another minute or so. If we break the connection too soon Nova will know something's up.'

'Wait, what's this?' Dylan yells, staring at the laptop. No, it can't be, no . . . no NOOOOO!!' she screams.

THE MYSTERIOUS
BLOSSOM

I run over to the laptop, there on the screen

is something that I can't get my head around.

Pictures of Courtney are slowly flashing up on

screen as they transfer to Nova, but they're not

ones I recognize. She looks like . . .

'A NERD!' Dylan yells.

Courtney goes pale. 'NO! No one was

supposed to see that ever!' she yells.

'Is that you?' I ask. 'Are you wearing braces

on your teeth? When was that picture taken? OMG. Are you part of a maths team?' I gasp out questions.

'This is exactly what I didn't want to happen!' Courtney says, slamming the laptop down.

'*That's* why you don't have a Nova. I thought it was strange,' Ashley says. 'It's because you have a dark secret past as a nerd. You're a geek, Courtney!'

'I am not!' Courtney roars. 'I was sent away for a while, I went to finishing school, got a makeover, had the braces on my teeth removed and changed my name.'

'Changed your name?' Dylan asks. 'From what?'

'Blossom,' Courtney sighs.

'*YOU* WERE BLOSSOM?' Dylan is gobsmacked. 'WE USED TO BE FRIENDS, WE HUNG OUT TOGETHER AT KINDERGARTEN, WE USED TO DO NUMBER PUZZLES!' She shakes her head. 'I thought you'd moved away or been kidnapped by aliens! All this time you were right here, in front of me!' Dylan rushes over and gives Courtney a hug. 'BLOSSOM!' she cries, squeezing her tightly.

'Get off, Dylan!' Courtney struggles.

'You do remember me!' Dylan squeals.

'Of course I do, I was pretending.' Courtney rolls her eyes. 'You remind me too much of the past. Blossom is dead. Long live Courtney! I'm so pleased my parents sent me to Switzerland for six months to study at a beauty school. Best thing they ever did!' Courtney beams.

'So, that's why you started school halfway through the year?' says Ashley.

'Yeah. Blossom disappeared, then six months later you turned up.' Dylan shakes her head.

'Blossom had to go.' Courtney sniffs. 'By helicopter, in the middle of the night.'

'It was a helicopter?' Dylan yells. 'That was the bright lights I remember? It wasn't a UFO!'

Courtney nods. 'It changed my life, and I've never been happier,' she says, with a smile that doesn't quite meet her eyes, which look sad and empty. 'And now that you realize my dark past, that's where it must stay.'

I tear myself away from this fascinating turn of events to look out of the window.

'I hate to interrupt this reunion, but that big sleepy monster outside . . . well, he's not so sleepy,' I mutter.

'Aw. You're still the same,' Dylan says, holding Blossom's hand. 'I can tell.'

'I AM NOT!'

'What's the square root of 169?' Dylan asks.

'Thirteen . . . I mean, I don't know. Look we don't have time for this!' Courtney-Blossom snaps.

'No, we really don't!' Ashley agrees.

'What's the seventh number after the decimal point of 206,754 divided by 3,536?'

Dylan asks, as Ashley dives across the room and pulls the plug out of the Wi-Fi modem.

'Stop it!' Courtney yells. Just at that second something smashes through the window. A spider claw surges into the house, grabs me, and pulls me outside.

It didn't work, people didn't turn their Wi-Fi off, we're doomed.

'FEED ME!' the monster screams in my face. So this is it. *This* is how I'm going to go— eaten by a spider robot? Suddenly I feel my stomach lurch as I'm lifted high in the air. I'm higher than the house, higher than the trees, and the spider robot opens its huge giant mouth and lets go. I begin to fall down towards a million little robot legs, that make up its teeth.

I close my eyes and hope for a quick end. But the end doesn't come. I sink to the ground, and slide onto the front of Courtney's drive on a wave of lifeless robot spiders.

It worked, the town did what it had to, it turned the Internet off. I stand up and look out to the town. People from all over are heading towards the house, with huge smiles on their faces. A second later I'm grabbed, but not by spider arms, it's Dylan, Ashley, and even Courtney pulling me into a hug.

There is a jubilant atmosphere as slowly but surely Courtney's drive fills up with people from around the town, cheering, hugging, and smashing up Novas. One by one the lights come back on, alarms stop buzzing, and what felt like a ghost town begins to feel normal again.

'The police are on their way!' Dad says, appearing in his car, which has been half munched by a Nova but just about works.

'Thanks, Courtney,' I say, holding out my hand.

She smiles, and shakes it. 'Any time.'

'Hey guys!' I say, climbing up onto a pile of now destroyed Novas. 'Thank you. I couldn't have done this without you, or Courtney. I'm sorry that this town got taken over by a giant man-eating robot spider, I really am, but in some ways I'm not. Look at what it did to us!' I say. 'We have jocks, nerds, cheerleaders, Happyville folk of every type working as one. Don't you see? All this about who's the best, who's the coolest. See what nonsense it is! We're all the same. I'm the same as Courtney, she's the same as me. Did you know she looked like me, once,' I shout to the crowd. There are a few murmurs of disbelief. 'I know. She's a secret nerd. And you know what, that's okay. If she wants to wear braces on her teeth and be good at maths, then why not? Maybe I can be a cheerleader too!' There are a few more murmurs. 'We can be anything we want to be, just as long as we're friends. And do you know what's brought us together in the end? No Internet. Maybe Happyville could be a no Internet zone, at least for some of the time. We can walk around, talk to each other, really get to know each other. Learn to love and get along with each other. With truth in our hearts, and happiness in our souls. Wouldn't you like that? Courtney, wouldn't you like to be who you really are? Be the geek that you were always meant to be?' I yell, looking from her to the sea of enthralled-looking faces.

'Or . . .' Courtney begins, 'We could turn the Wi-Fi back on? It's been ten minutes now, and the Novas are destroyed. We can go and watch that new reality show that's tearing up Amazon?'

To this there is huge amounts of cheering and whooping and Courtney shrugs. 'Sorry!' she says to me, with a smile. 'Oh, and if anyone ever shows anyone else or even talks about that picture of me as Blossom, I'll kill you all, stone dead.'

'Really, you're going to threaten us?' Ashley asks.

'Yes. I know everything about anyone and everyone in this town, so don't try me,' Courtney winks. 'This town has only got room for one Nova.'

'Budge up!' Dad says, bringing us a plate of rice crackers.

'Shouldn't you be writing something?' Ashley asks him, as we all settle down to watch *Antiques Goldmine*.

'Not today. What I don't do this evening I'll do tomorrow.' Dad grins. 'Plus I want to see what the fuss is about with this show,' he says, picking up the remote.

'I see they've changed the sponsors,'

Dylan says.

'Well they had to, now that all the Novas have been taken off the shelf due to "technical problems".'

We watch as a brand new advert comes on before the show.

'Hi. When I'm not acting or modelling, I like to teach. And the best way to teach is by looking good! That's why I use Orangu-tan—a spray tan that gives me a totally natural yet luminous glow.'

'MR JONES!' we all gasp.

'Uh-oh,' Ashley says, going green. 'Sorry, I'm allergic to stonewashed denim, even the sight of it makes me—'

'COME ON ASH!' Dylan cries, 'THIS WAY!'
They scamper off from the living room to try
and find a toilet in time.

'Thanks for the snacks, Dad, you didn't
need to do this,' I smile, slapping on some
peanut butter.

'I like to! There
are some things a
computer can't do!'
he says, giving me
a hug.

OTHER BOOKS BY
Tom McLaughlin

THE Accidental
PRIME MINISTER

"HATS FOR CATS!"

Tom McLaughlin

THE Accidental
FATHER CHRISTMAS

IT'S A
CRACKER!

Tom McLaughlin

HAPPYVILLE HIGH

GEEK
TRAGEDY

TOO UNCOOL FOR SCHO

TOM McLAUGH

THE Accidental
ROCK STAR

IT'S A
HIT!

Tom McLaughlin

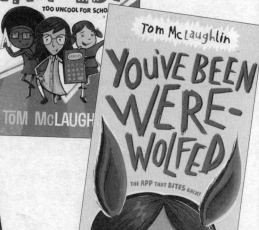

Tom McLaughlin

YOU'VE BEEN
WERE-
WOLFED

THE APP THAT BITES BACK!

ABOUT THE AUTHOR

Before becoming a writer and illustrator Tom
spent nine years working as political cartoonist
for *The Western Morning News* thinking up
silly jokes about even sillier politicians. Then, in
2004 Tom took the plunge into illustrating and
writing his own books. Since then he has written
and illustrated picture books and fiction as well
as working on animated TV shows for Disney and
Cartoon Network.

Tom lives in Devon and his hobbies include
drinking tea, looking out of the window, and
biscuits. His hates include spiders and running
out of tea and biscuits.